DISNEP

AGENT
STITCH

THE TROUBLE WITH TOOTHOIDS

For Nina, who I met in New York City
—S.B.

Published by Disney Press, an imprint of Buena Vista Books, Inc. No part of this book may be reproduced or transmitted in any form or by any means, electronic or mechanical, including photocopying, recording, or by any information storage and retrieval system, without written permission from the publisher. For information address Disney Press, 1200 Grand Central Avenue, Glendale, California 91201.

First Hardcover Edition, May 2023
1 3 5 7 9 10 8 6 4 2
FAC-038091-23104
ISBN 978-1-368-07133-8
Printed in the United States of America
Library of Congress Control Number: 2021949331
Visit disneybooks.com

SUSTAINABLE FORESTRY INITIATIVE   Certified Sourcing

www.forests.org
SFI-01268

Logo Applies to Text Stock Only

THE TROUBLE WITH TOOTHOIDS

Written by **STEVE BEHLING**

Illustrated by **ARIANNA REA**

DISNEP PRESS

LOS ANGELES · NEW YORK

CLASSIFIED FILE

GALACTIC DETECTIVE AGENCY

Full Name: Stitch

Aliases: Agent 626, Experiment 626

Distinguishing Features: Four arms, two of which can be retracted into subject's body; retractable antennae; back spines

Planet of Origin: Unknown (Dr. Jumba Jookiba has yet to reveal full details of creature's origin)

Present Location: E-arth

Occupation: Abomination, dog, detective

Known Associates: Lilo Pelekai, Nani Pelekai, Dr. Jumba Jookiba, Pleakley

Background: Created by Dr. Jumba Jookiba, Experiment 626 was initially captured by the Galactic Federation and exiled to a deserted asteroid. Subject now lives on E-arth as part of the Pelekai family, under the protection of the Grand Councilwoman.

A series of strange events in the E-arth city of Paris, France, caused the Grand Councilwoman to enlist Experiment 626 as an agent of the Galactic Detective Agency. His efforts (along with those of his colleagues Lilo Pelekai, Jookiba, and Agent Pleakley) and his investigation into this situation exposed and thwarted a plot by the Snailiens to conquer E-arth.

CLASSIFIED FILE

GALACTIC DETECTIVE AGENCY

Full Name: Pelekai, Lilo

Aliases: None known

Distinguishing Features: Incredible cuteness disguising great bravery, inner strength

Planet of Origin: E-arth

Present Location: E-arth

Occupation: Human child

Known Associates: Nani Pelekai (sister), Stitch, Dr. Jumba Jookiba, Pleakley, Scrump*

Background: Lilo Pelekai is a young girl who was born and raised on the planet E-arth and lives with her sister (Nani) and Experiment 626, aka Stitch. Subject accompanied Agent 626 to Paris, where her remarkable grit, intelligence, and refusal to give up proved invaluable in the successful resolution of the Snailien affair. It is highly recommended that subject continue to work with Agent 626. She is well on her way to being a stellar GDA agent herself.

---

* NOTE: We have so far been unable to learn anything about this "Scrump". Suggest Agent Peebles look into this unknown entity immediately.

CLASSIFIED FILE

×

GALACTIC DETECTIVE AGENCY

Full Name: Jookiba, Dr. Jumba

Aliases: Unknown

Distinguishing Features: Four eyes

Planet of Origin: Quelte Quan

Present Location: E-arth

Occupation: Scientist, mad

Known Associates: Pleakley, Stitch, Lilo Pelekai, Nani Pelekai, Experiments 1–625

Background: Dr. Jumba Jookiba (degree obtained from Evil Genius University) conducted a series of unauthorized, highly illegal experiments involving the creation of creatures. Subject now lives with the Pelekai family, and he accompanied Agent 626 on the Paris investigation. Though he spent a good deal of that time inside the belly of a large Snailien, he eventually helped resolve the situation and defeat the Snailiens. For such a brilliant scientist, he does amazingly little science, but the Grand Councilwoman says that's for the best.

CLASSIFIED

CLASSIFIED FILE

GALACTIC DETECTIVE AGENCY

Full Name: Pleakley, Wendy

Aliases: Agent Pleakley (former)

Distinguishing Features: One eye, three legs, obvious yet tasteful wig

Planet of Origin: Plorgonar

Present Location: E-arth

Occupation: Former agent of the Galactic Federation; mosquito expert

Known Associates: Dr. Jumba Jookiba, Stitch, Lilo Pelekai, Nani Pelekai, wig

Background: Former agent Pleakley spent a good deal of his career working for the Galactic Federation. He was chiefly known as an expert on a species of insects called mosquitoes, from the planet E-arth. Like Dr. Jookiba, Pleakley spent a substantial amount of time during the Paris affair trapped inside the stomach of a huge Snailien. According to the report, Pleakley's so-called wig was largely responsible for their escape. It is the GDA's recommendation that Pleakley have a steady supply of these E-arth wigs handy, as they seem to be most useful.

GALACTIC DETECTIVE AGENCY
OFFICIAL HANDBOOK

GALACTIC DETECTIVE AGENCY RULES ✕

RULE #1
Wherever you go, look for clues.

RULE #2
Collect evidence, but don't touch it or
you'll spoil it.

RULE #3
A good detective knows when to
detect—and when to run.

RULE #4
Be patient! Don't rush into a situation.

RULE #5
When in doubt, spit it out.

RULE #6
Just because something appears
obvious, that doesn't mean it isn't true.

RULE #7
Be resourceful. Use what you have
around you to your advantage.

RULE #8
Always take a closer look: you may
notice something new.

RULE #9
Have a plan! (Even if it's not a great
plan, it's still better than no plan.)

RULE #10
Sometimes you just have to
unleash your inner stitch!

New York City was known as the city that never sleeps.*

There was always something going on in this bustling metropolis, regardless of the time of day. Morning, noon, or night, people hustled about, going from one place to another, racing from home to their jobs, or out to meet friends, or to enjoy a brisk walk through the city's famed Central Park.

* Of course cities don't sleep. They don't need sleep. People need sleep. It should be called "the city that never sleeps because it doesn't have to but the people who live there sure need some rest."**
** This is probably too wordy for a slogan.

And the easiest way to get to any of those places was the subway. A series of underground trains that ran up, down, and across the city's five boroughs, including the island of Manhattan, the subway could take a person practically anywhere they wanted to go.

So it wasn't at all strange to see people walking around, at any time of day, entering any of the city's 472 subway stations.

What *was* strange was how one particular woman stared straight ahead, as if she was looking through the crowd of people coming up and down the stairs at the Fourteenth Street and Seventh Avenue subway entrance. She ran right into a surly man walking a grunting bulldog past an overflowing trash can.

"Why don't you watch where you're going?" the surly man complained as the curious bulldog sniffed at the trash can.

But the woman didn't notice the surly man at all. It was like she wasn't even on the same planet! She just looked ahead, her eyes glassy.

"Going to the subway, lots of work to do," she

said to herself. "Trek through the tunnels, beneath the avenue."

"What's that?" the man asked. "You a poet or somethin'?"

The woman didn't react, but she kept on talking. "Drip-drip goes the water, as we keep on rhyming. Watch the garden grow, isn't it enlightening?"

The surly man bit his lip. "Weirdo," he said, and the bulldog tilted her head and growled.

At last the woman began walking again, and she disappeared down the subway stairs.

"This city is full of weirdos," the surly man said, then turned to the bulldog, who was still sniffing the trash can. "Ain't that right, Ms. Muggins?"

Ms. Muggins snarled in reply, shoving her body against the surly man, forcing him away from the garbage.

"What, now you're actin' weird, too?" the surly man asked. He watched as the bulldog picked up something off the ground in her mouth.

"What is that? Get that outta yer mouth! You don't know where it's been!" the man said as he reached in. He pulled a long, spiky object from between Ms. Muggins's teeth.

Unexpectedly, the trash can moved forward, closer to Ms. Muggins and the man. The garbage inside expanded as the trash can grew larger and larger. Sitting on top of the can was a small green metal box.

"What the—" the surly man said, dropping the spike. But that was all he could manage before a beam of light flashed from the green box.

The man's complaining stopped immediately, and he became quiet.

His eyes glazed over, and he let go of Ms. Muggins's leash and followed the moving trash can down the stairs, in the same direction as the weird woman had gone.

The helpless dog could only bark as the surly man said, "Going to the subway . . . lots of work to do. Trek through the tunnels, beneath the avenue. . . ."

HOLD IT!

HOLD EVERYTHING!

WHAT'S WRONG WITH BEING A WEIRDO?
Isn't *everyone* a little weird sometimes?

◻ YES

Excellent. I'm glad we could agree on that!
Anyway, even if everyone is a little weird
sometimes, what just happened was
particularly weird, wouldn't you agree?

◻ It seems like I should say yes, so yes.

Double excellent! Then you're ready to turn
the page and delve into Agent 626's latest case,
which we like to call . . .

~~Stitch's Totally Awesome New York City~~ Exploits!

The Trouble with Toothoids!

(a little more dramatic than the other title)

CHAPTER 1

CONFIDENTIAL

CRASH LANDING

CONFIDENTIAL

Meanwhile, somewhere over the Atlantic Ocean . . .

"Somewhere over the Atlantic Ocean" covers a lot of ground, doesn't it? Sorry, it doesn't actually cover any ground on account of all the water. What I should have said is "'Somewhere over the Atlantic Ocean' covers a lot of water, doesn't it?"

You know what? It just occurred to me that this book isn't called *The Difference Between Ground and Water*—it's *Agent Stitch*, right? That means the sooner we get to Stitch, Lilo, Jumba, and Pleakley, the better. Sorry for the delay.

"I miss Paris," Pleakley said as he looked out the RV window wistfully. "Doesn't it seem like we were there only an hour ago?"

"We *were* there only an hour ago," Jumba replied. "Had whole adventure there, remember?"

"Of course I remember the adventure! It was fun!" Pleakley protested, folding his arms and sticking out his lower lip. "I got stuck inside the stomach of a big gooey Snailien with my best friend! How can I forget?"

"I don't remember that moment as being especially fun," Jumba retorted.

"Well, individuals can remember things differently, I guess," Pleakley replied curtly. He seemed miffed at Jumba, who didn't even acknowledge that Pleakley had called him his best friend.

"Hey, can you guys keep it down?" Lilo said. "Stitch is trying to fly the RV, and your bickering is distracting him."

"It's okay," Stitch said as he pulled back on the wheel of the RV. The vehicle zoomed ahead, soaring over the Atlantic Ocean. "Stitch knows how to ignore Jumba."

"I heard that!" Jumba said.

"I think you were supposed to," Lilo replied, grinning at Jumba and Pleakley.

Now hold on just a second. I know what you're saying: "Who are these 'Snailien' characters? What were Stitch and his friends even doing in Paris to begin with? Also, why doesn't this book come with ice cream?"

Well, I'm with you on the ice cream. As far as I'm concerned, *every* book should come with ice cream. But that's neither here nor there.

So let's back it up for a bit. The thing you need to know about Stitch is he's an alien who began his life as a scientific experiment—Experiment 626, to be exact. Initially running afoul of the Galactic Federation, he established a new life on the planet known as E-arth, taking refuge in Hawai'i with a little girl named Lilo and her big sister, Nani. Keeping them company was Dr. Jumba Jookiba, the genius scientist who had created Stitch, and Pleakley, a . . . well, I guess he's a mosquito expert. Watching over them was a social worker named Cobra Bubbles, who was also an agent with the Galactic Federation.

Everything was going just fine. And then, one day, Nani suggested that Lilo and Stitch take a road trip around the island of Kaua'i with Jumba and Pleakley. The Grand Councilwoman chose that moment to recruit Stitch for the Galactic Detective Agency (that's the GDA), to uncover a mystery in Paris, France.

This was an assignment Stitch took seriously. How seriously?

Moreover, Stitch wanted to prove to the Grand Councilwoman that he could be a really good agent and an absolutely stellar detective and help solve all kinds of problems.

Dubbed Agent 626 by the Grand Councilwoman, Stitch flew to Paris with his companions, on the sticky trail of an alien species known as the Snailiens. Along with Lilo, Jumba, Pleakley, Agent Cobra Bubbles, and a good Snailien named

Flootbar,* Agent 626 fought the Snailien leader, Zoolox the Unreasonable. Zoolox was obsessed with invading E-arth and "UHOP," which was a pancake place or something. The group fought Zoolox atop the Eiffel Tower and succeeded in preventing the bad guys from invading E-arth via a type of alien technology known as the IMDARB (short for Inter-Molecular Disassembly and Reassembly Beam).

Along the way, Stitch learned about the detective rules created by the GDA, which all agents should follow. He even added one of his own! And if you don't believe me, just turn to the beginning of the book, where the rules are listed.

Upon the completion of their mission, the Grand Councilwoman informed Agent 626 that there was trouble in New York City and directed him to meet Cobra Bubbles, another GDA operative, who had traveled ahead to begin the investigation.

Okay, so now you're all caught up. Where were we? Oh, right!

---

* Yes, Flootbar was also the alien who tried to eat Jumba and Pleakley. But that was before he decided to help our friends.

"Stitch, are we getting close to New York City?" Lilo asked.

"Very close," Stitch said as he pointed at the skyline filled with buildings, ahead.

"Now be careful," Lilo said. "You need to find a place big enough to set the RV down where we won't hurt anybody. Maybe somewhere here. . . ."

Lilo pulled up a map on the RV's control screen.

Stitch scoffed. He had worked hard on their Paris mission to prove that he could be an agent, and he had done it! So surely he could land a flying RV without any help, too. After all, he was a full-fledged agent of the GDA—and this was *his* mission!

"Stitch knows where to land," he said, maybe a little too confidently.

"But, Stitch, you've never been to New York City, and—" Lilo protested.

"Little girl may be right," Jumba said.

"Agreed!" Pleakley chimed in.

Despite his friends' protests, Stitch wanted to show them that he knew exactly what he was doing. He was the leader of the group, wasn't he?

"Get ready for landing!" Stitch said with authority.

"Hold on tight!" Stitch said as he activated the reverse-thrust mechanisms located on the underside of the RV. They allowed the vehicle to take off and land vertically. The RV burst through

some wispy clouds right over Central Park and descended rapidly toward the lawn. Stitch had his sights set on landing the RV on the shores of Turtle Pond, which was named for—you guessed it—the large number of turtles that inhabited the area.

But the RV was still coming in too quickly! Stitch attempted to put on the air brakes, but it was too little, too late. The RV overshot the grassy area at the shore of Turtle Pond and crashed right into the water!

SPLASH!

THE MISSION

It was the middle of the afternoon, and people were outside, taking in the fresh air and sunshine. Some were lounging on picnic blankets, enjoying a late lunch. Others were walking dogs or playing softball. And because this was New York City, nobody seemed to care that a flying RV had splashed down into Turtle Pond—except for one person, who wore a dark suit and equally dark sunglasses. He walked right past the picnickers and dog walkers and softball players, stopped by the shore of the pond, and waited.

Stitch stared out the window at the water that surrounded the RV. He was supposed to land the vehicle on the shore, not in the water! He felt embarrassed by his mistake. He had only himself to blame, and he knew it. But he was the leader. He couldn't admit that he had been wrong, could he?

"I meant to do that," Stitch lied. "Cool off the engines."

"Stitch, why didn't you listen to me?" Lilo asked.

Stitch didn't answer. He just wanted to pretend everything was fine. So he rolled down the window and jumped out.

"No, Stitch!" Lilo said.

But it was too late, and Stitch was already out the window. He hit the water and immediately began to sink. He hadn't counted on the pond being so deep! Stitch's body was so dense that upon contact with water, he just plummeted!

The same thing had happened to him back in Hawai'i. He had gone surfing one day with Lilo, Nani, and Nani's friend David. Stitch fell off the board and sank immediately. Ultimately, David was able to rescue him.

And now here he was, sinking beneath the surface of Turtle Pond.

A second later, Stitch felt a massive hand on his shoulder.

With a yank, Stitch reappeared above the surface, soaking wet. He saw Cobra Bubbles standing next to him, holding him up with both hands.

"You're surprisingly heavy," Cobra said, "and right on time."

"A good detective is always on time," Agent 626 said, spitting out water. That actually sounded like a pretty good detective rule, so he made a mental note to start adding his own rules to the official list.

STITCH'S DETECTIVE RULE #11

A good detective is always on time.

"*Stitch, what were you thinking?*" Lilo said, climbing out of the RV toward them. "You have to be more careful! You could have been hurt! We all could have been hurt, or you could have injured someone down on the ground!"

"Stitch knew what he was doing all along," he said, trying to cover up for his error. "Everything turned out fine. Right, team?"

The sound of the RV taking off drowned out Stitch's voice. At the controls, Jumba flew the vehicle out of Turtle Pond and landed it on the shore.

Before Stitch could say anything more, Cobra spoke.

"I'm glad you're here," Cobra said. "It's only been a short while, but a lot's happened since I saw you in Paris. And none of it's good."

"What's going on?" Lilo asked.

Cobra gave a quick nod, then turned the dial of his watch. "I'll let *her* tell you."

The Grand Councilwoman appeared above the watch dial in a hologram projection.

She was really light-years away, on her ship orbiting the planet Turo, headquarters to the Galactic Federation as well as the Galactic Detective Agency. Behind her, seated at a console, was a small pink alien entering data into a large computer.

"Agent Bubbles, Agent 626, the situation is direr than we thought," the Grand Councilwoman began. "You will need to work together if you are to successfully solve this case. Agent 626, I trust you'll follow Agent Bubbles's lead."

Immediately, Stitch bristled. He had thought this was supposed to be his mission. Why was she putting Cobra in charge now? Stitch didn't like it, not one bit—not after he had proven himself in Paris.

"Excuse me," Stitch said, "but Stitch—"

"We'll have time for questions later, 626," the Grand Councilwoman said.

Stitch grumbled, nodding. Not only couldn't he lead the team all on his own now, but he wasn't even allowed to speak?

"For this particular assignment, your main contact will be Agent Peebles. They'll be handling all communication, while I review the details of the Snailien affair. You all remember Agent Peebles," the Grand Councilwoman said, gesturing toward the pink alien.

You will not be remotely surprised that no one remembered Agent Peebles.

"No," Jumba said, answering for everyone. "No, we don't."

"Oh," the Grand Councilwoman replied. "Well, of *course* you remember Agent Peebles. They were present during your first briefing on the Snailiens!"

See, Peebles was there!

"Nope, still nothing," Jumba said.

"I have been here the whole time!" Agent Peebles finally spoke up. "Remember? I was also there when the Grand Councilwoman told you to go to New York."

Peebles was there, too!

"It honestly doesn't ring a bell," Pleakley said.

"Regardless," the Grand Councilwoman continued, "Agent Peebles is my special assistant, and they have my complete trust. Anything you would say to me, you can say to them."

Stitch nodded.

"Now, I must stress that the information we're about to share with you must be kept secret," the Grand Councilwoman intoned. "Agent Peebles, will you please deliver the report?"

"Of course, Grand Councilwoman," Agent Peebles said. "During the last week, the GDA has received intelligence of people in New York City falling into some kind of trance. Almost immediately, they head for the nearest subway station, where they disappear into the tunnels . . . never to be seen again!"

"Oh, very dramatic delivery," Jumba said, impressed.

"Curiously, while entranced, these individuals seem to communicate almost exclusively in"—Agent Peebles gave a long pause—"*rhyme.*"

"Again with the dramatic delivery," Jumba muttered.

"We have no direct visual evidence of one of these incidents," Agent Peebles said. "But our experts here have done a reenactment so you can better understand what we're dealing with."

They pushed a button, and a prerecorded video played on the hologram.

"Well, that was terrifying," Lilo said once the video ended.

"Virtually the only evidence we've been able to recover," the Grand Councilwoman said, "is this."

She held up what looked like a spike of some sort. It was almost like a tooth. "It's not of Earth," the Grand Councilwoman continued. "But our scientists have so far been unable to determine the species to which it belongs. The DNA contained in the spike appears to keep . . . changing."

"Impossible," Jumba said flatly.

"Why is that impossible?" Lilo asked.

"Because only galaxy's most brilliant scientist could accomplish such a thing," Jumba insisted. "And since I am galaxy's most brilliant scientist and I haven't done it yet, it is therefore impossible!"

The Grand Councilwoman rolled her eyes. "And yet it is so. Based on this evidence, we suspect the involvement of an as-yet-unknown alien species. Their motives and goals for manipulating the humans remains a mystery—a mystery that I hope you and Agent Bubbles can solve, 626."

Stitch saluted the hologram of the Grand Councilwoman. "Agent 626 is on the case!"

"Of course you are," replied the Grand Councilwoman, pleased. "Now, unlike your previous assignment involving the Snailiens, we have no idea who's responsible. That means we don't know their abilities or their weaknesses."

"That's not so good," Lilo chimed in. "We're going to have to stick together on this one, Stitch."

Then she gave Stitch a look that said, *I mean it.*

Stitch scowled.

"Your assignment is as follows," the Grand Councilwoman said.

×

GALACTIC DETECTIVE AGENCY
Assignment # XPG–31003.45
AGENTS ASSIGNED TO CASE:

Cobra Bubbles   626

☐ OBJECTIVE 1: Uncover the aliens responsible.

☐ OBJECTIVE 2: Find out the aliens' plans.

☐ OBJECTIVE 3: Put a stop to the aliens' plans.

"Agent 626, I understand that you've already received a pair of GLURBs from Agent Bubbles," the Grand Councilwoman added.

Stitch tilted his head curiously. "GLURBs?" he asked.

"Galactic Laser-Utilizing Refraction Bifocals," Cobra replied. "These."

Then he pointed at the dark glasses he wore.

"Too confusing. Why not just say 'glasses' instead of 'GLURBs'?" Jumba asked.

Stitch ignored Jumba *again* and took out the pair of GLURBs Cobra had given to him upon the completion of their Snailien case. He put the glasses* on.

"Those glasses can detect the presence of unknown aliens," Cobra explained. "To activate them, all you have to do is . . ."

And Cobra explained in great detail exactly how to switch on the "Scan for Alien" feature, which would have been great if Stitch had actually been listening. The reason he wasn't listening—or wasn't able to listen—was that . . . Well, I'll just show you.

---

* Sorry, we mean GLURBs. Jumba was right: that *is* confusing.

"Do we all get GLURBs?" asked Lilo, who had been listening intently to Cobra's instructions.

"An excellent question, Lilo," the Grand Councilwoman said. "The plan *was* to equip you all with GLURBs to aid you on this case. However . . ."

The Grand Councilwoman turned to face Agent Peebles, who grimaced.

"The, ah, shipment of GLURBs that was intended for you was accidentally IMDARBed to the planet Noodelon Six."

"Noodelon Six?" Lilo asked.

"The sixth farthest noodle planet from the Galactic Center of the Universe," Agent Peebles explained.

"Unfortunate," Jumba said.

"Yes, unfortunate," Agent Peebles repeated as the Grand Councilwoman glared at them. "And, um, my fault."

"Well, we mustn't dwell on past mistakes," the Grand Councilwoman said. "Agent 626, we will need to update your detective tools as well. We're sending those to you now via IMDARB."

There was a sudden glimmer of light blasting

onto the ground right in front of the group. When the flash disappeared, there was a small gold case. It resembled the silver case that was part of Stitch's Detective Tool Belt, which he had received during the previous assignment.

And sitting on the ground next to the case were five circular devices.

"This will replace your old set of tools," the Grand Councilwoman said. "Inside, you'll find items we think you may find useful. I've also sent you each a new galactic communicator. Agent 626, Agent Bubbles, Lilo, Jumba, Pleakley—take one, please. That way you can remain in constant contact."

Stitch nodded as the Grand Councilwoman said, "You have your mission. Good luck, agents."

Stitch watched as the hologram of the Grand Councilwoman faded away.

CHAPTER 3

CONFIDENTIAL

TURTLE TALK

CONFIDENTIAL

"So where do we start?" Jumba asked the group. He felt something tap against his toes, and he looked down to see a small turtle repeatedly bumping its head against his foot.

Hello, little fellow.

"I think that turtle really likes you," Lilo observed.

"Never mind the turtle," Cobra said. "I've got a lead. But it's a slim one."

"What is it?" Lilo asked.

"Before you arrived, I saw something . . . odd," Cobra replied. "I mean *odd*."

Then Cobra turned the dial on his watch again, and another hologram appeared. It showed a woman walking down the stairs toward a subway station, her eyes glazed over. In front of her was a bicycle, moving without a rider.

"A bicycle riding itself?" Stitch asked. Since he had come to Earth, Stitch hadn't had a lot of experience riding bicycles. Not any, in fact. But he had seen Lilo and her sister, Nani, ride them back home in Hawai'i. He knew that bicycles didn't usually, if ever, ride themselves.

"Yeah, that's not something you see every day," Cobra added.

"Why is that lady just walking behind the bike?" Lilo wondered. "She seems kind of . . . weird."

"That's the million-dollar question," Cobra said. "Her eyes look glassy, almost like she's in a trance.

Apparently, she followed the bicycle down into the subway."

"But these people on the stairs," Jumba said as the turtle bumped up against his foot again, "are they not bothered by phantom bicycle? Does possible existence of ghosts not strike fear into their hearts?"

"There's no such thing as ghosts, at least as far as I know," Cobra said. "Besides, we're talking about New Yorkers here. They see strange things every day. They're used to it."

"I see strange things every day, too," Jumba said, pointing at Pleakley. "I am *not* used to it."

Stitch thought for a moment and then pressed the center of his Galactic Detective Agency badge. A hologram of the *GDA Official Handbook* appeared, and Stitch turned right to the section marked *CLUES*. Then he swiped at the top of the hologram as he made an entry.

CLUES

1. Rhyming??
2. weird tooth?
3. Lady in trance
4. Bicycle—rides itself. very strange.

"Where did this happen?" Lilo asked.

"Yes," Stitch said, trying to assert himself. He pushed himself in front of Lilo and faced Cobra directly. "Where did this happen?"

"At Grand Central Terminal," Cobra said, "one

of the largest transportation hubs in this city. The moment I saw the bicycle, and the woman following it, I obviously knew something wasn't right. I attempted to 'Scan for Alien' with my GLURBs. But before I could get a definitive reading, the bicycle and the woman went down to the subway tracks and crossed over them, toward the wall. A second later, a train pulled into the station and blocked them from sight."

"And then?" Jumba asked, interested. The little turtle bonked its head against his foot once more. He glanced down at the creature and said, "My, but you are persistent."

"Doors opened. People got off the train. People got on. Then the train pulled away. And when it was gone, both the woman and the bicycle had vanished," Cobra said.

Stitch continued to take notes furiously.

"What do you think, everyone?" Lilo asked.

Stitch cleared his throat, so the group turned to look at him as he finished his notes. Then he tapped the center of his GDA badge. The hologram disappeared, and Stitch held a paw to his chin. "Stitch thinks," he said, "we go to Grand Central Terminal!"

Then Stitch checked the new Detective Tool Belt that had been given to him by the Grand Councilwoman. Like the tool belt he'd had back in Paris, this one had a case that seemed to be bigger on the inside than it was on the outside. Stitch had no idea how much it could hold or precisely what was stored in it. He just knew that when he reached in, he could generally find something useful.

Stitch pulled out what looked like a compass. It had indicators for north, south, east, and west, and all the directions in between.

"Omni-compass," Cobra observed. "All you have to do to use it is—"

"Stitch knows how," Stitch said, pulling the compass closer.

Then Stitch looked for buttons to press on the omni-compass, but there weren't any. So he started to shake it.

And . . . nothing happened.

"It doesn't work like that," Cobra said. Then he spoke into the omni-compass. "Take us to Grand Central Terminal."

A voice from the compass said, "Follow me!"

The device beeped and indicated for the group to walk south.

"How cool is that?" Lilo said.

"Meh," was all Stitch could manage. He narrowed his eyes at Cobra.

As everyone left, Jumba noticed the turtle was now sitting on his foot. Very gently, he reached down, picked up the turtle, and set it on a rock right at the edge of the pond.

"Here you go, little fellow," Jumba said. Following Stitch and the group, Jumba headed south, toward Grand Central Terminal.

If they had bothered to turn around, they would have seen the little turtle sitting on the rock, sneering as Stitch and his friends departed, and cackling in a most evil, un-turtle-like way as its body slowly changed shape . . .

. . . into a bicycle.

CHAPTER 4

CONFIDENTIAL

THE SUBWAY

CONFIDENTIAL

It's about a forty-five-minute walk from the Turtle Pond in Central Park to Grand Central Terminal, give or take. Stitch and company took a little over an hour, but that's only because there were some . . . let's call them *incidents* . . . that happened along the way. Admittedly, most of these incidents could have been avoided if it weren't for a certain one-eyed alien. Take a look at the next page and you'll see what we mean.

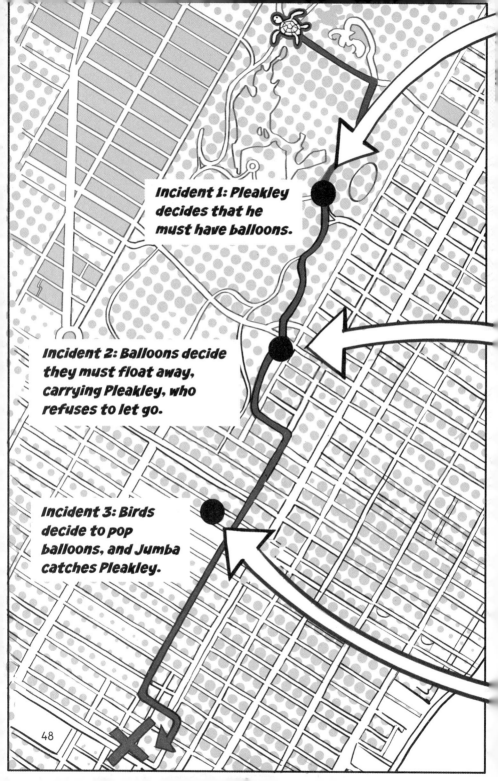

Incident 1: Pleakley decides that he must have balloons.

Incident 2: Balloons decide they must float away, carrying Pleakley, who refuses to let go.

Incident 3: Birds decide to pop balloons, and Jumba catches Pleakley.

"No more balloons for you," Jumba said as the group neared its destination. The whole walk south, Jumba seemed to be getting increasingly annoyed with Pleakley's antics.

"It could have happened to anybody," Pleakley protested weakly.

"It didn't happen to 'anybody,'" Cobra replied, exasperated. "It happened to *you*. Also, what are you doing with that book?"

Cobra pointed at a book Pleakley had tucked into his dress. Pleakley pulled it out to show everyone.

"I picked it up before I got the balloons," Pleakley said. "This book is amazing! It tells you all the fun things you can do in the Big Apple, which I haven't seen yet, but it must be around here somewhere. I wonder just how big the apple is!"

Stitch ignored Pleakley. He knew that a detective had to keep focused on the task at hand, especially if he was going to lead his team. Again, this struck him as a pretty good detective rule, so he wrote it down.

STITCH'S DETECTIVE RULE #12
Stay focused on the task at hand— even when Pleakley is rambling.

Stitch and his friends opened the doors to Grand Central Terminal on Forty-Fifth Street between Park and Lexington Avenues, then walked down a long hallway, passing through a crowd of busy people coming and going. Stitch was enjoying his time in New York City so far. He hadn't even bothered to go into dog mode, because New Yorkers didn't seem to care that a furry blue alien was in their midst. It was awesome!

The omni-compass announced, "You have arrived at your destination," and Stitch put it back inside his Detective Tool Belt.

He was just about to head down a corridor when Cobra said, "Follow me."

Agent 626 glared at Cobra, watching as the agent headed into another hallway and down a flight of stairs. Jumba and Pleakley followed him.

When Lilo saw that Stitch wasn't walking, she said, "C'mon, we have to go! Cobra needs us!"

Grumbling, Stitch said, "Stitch is coming."

Then he followed Lilo and the others.

Soon they came to a stand of turnstiles, where people taking the trains had to slide a card to pay their fare. Cobra produced one of these cards and slid it through a card reader on a turnstile.

"You first," Cobra said, and Stitch went through. Cobra swiped the card again, and Lilo entered. Then he swiped for Jumba.

"You coming or not?" Cobra asked when he noticed Pleakley was holding on to a nearby pole.

"I'm not going through that thing!" Pleakley said. "Who knows what could happen?"

"I went through it, and I'm a kid!" Lilo said, smiling.

"I went through it, and I'm genius scientist," Jumba said, also smiling.

Cobra lowered his glasses and rolled his eyes. "I don't have time for this."

Then Stitch scrambled under the turnstile and pried Pleakley's hands off the pole. He lifted the one-eyed alien over his head and nodded at Cobra. Agent Bubbles swiped his card and Stitch carried Pleakley through the turnstile.

"See?" Stitch said. "Nothing to be afraid of."

"Huh," Pleakley replied. "I'm braver than I thought!"

Cobra swiped the card again and entered behind the others. "This is the platform," he said. "And look down at those tracks. *That's* where I lost the bicycle."

Stitch nodded and reached into his Detective
Tool Belt. He pulled out a magnifying glass and
peered through it. The lens telescoped out until
it reached the very spot on the tracks where the
bicycle had gone missing.

"Hmmm," Stitch said.

"Be careful, Stitch," Lilo reminded her friend. "You don't want to get too close to the tracks. It's dangerous."

"She's right," Cobra said.

Stitch looked at Lilo and then at Cobra and huffed. Why couldn't they understand that he knew what he was doing? He was about to say something when Cobra's Galactic Detective Badge began to ring.

Cobra pressed the center. "Agent Bubbles," he said. "What have you got?"

"Agent Peebles with some important information," came the voice on the other end. "Apparently, there's been another sighting."

"Where, and what?" Cobra asked with intensity.

"The 'where' is downtown," Agent Peebles replied. "I'll send you the coordinates. And the 'what' is several garbage cans."

Cobra almost laughed, but not quite. "That seems . . . unremarkable."

"You didn't let me finish," Agent Peebles said. "Several garbage cans have been spotted downtown . . . herding a group of people into a subway station."

"Huh, that's a bit more remarkable," Cobra replied.

Agent Peebles sent the coordinates, then the transmission ended.

"Okay!" Stitch said, seizing the moment. "We need to go—"

"Hold on," Cobra said, interrupting Stitch. "'We' aren't going anywhere. Just me. *I'll* check out this lead. It could be dangerous. And I think we'd both agree that I have more experience when it comes to this kind of thing."

Stitch bristled.

"You keep investigating here, Stitch," Cobra continued. "See if you can dig up any clues about that missing woman and the bicycle. Everyone, be careful. Take care of each other, and we'll meet up later. I'll contact you over the GDA badge. Understood?"

"Understood," Lilo said.

Jumba and Pleakley both nodded.

But Stitch didn't say or do anything.

"Agent 626?" Cobra said, lowering his glasses and making eye contact. "Are we good?"

At last Stitch looked up at Cobra. He was tired of everyone treating him like he couldn't do anything alone. He knew he could be a leader and every bit as good an agent as Cobra.

But Cobra had said Stitch wasn't experienced enough. How was Stitch supposed to get experience if no one let him do anything? In that moment, Stitch resolved that he would show everyone *exactly* what he could do by himself.

"Understood," Stitch finally said. He gave Cobra a sharp nod as he watched the agent run toward the subway exit.

Once Cobra had left, Stitch began to scour the subway platform with his magnifying glass, searching for clues. Then he began to call out orders to the others.

"Jumba! You check over there!" he said, pointing at a bench.

The scientist turned to Stitch with a questioning look on his face and said, "But what does bench have to do with—"

"Pleakley! Help Jumba investigate bench!" Stitch continued.

Pleakley blinked several times. "Excuse me, but I think Jumba might actually be right—"

"Just do it!" Stitch exclaimed, frustration filling his voice.

"All right, all right," Jumba said. "So insistent."

Then the scientist looked at Pleakley. "And what do you mean 'Jumba *might* actually be right'? I am *always* right!"

Pleakley rolled his eye as a look of concern crossed Lilo's face.

She walked to Stitch and put a hand on his back. "What's wrong?" she asked. "Why are you acting like this?"

"Acting?" Stitch replied. "Acting like what? Stitch is fine."

"I know you, Stitch," Lilo said. "And something's not right. The way you were just now with Jumba and Pleakley? You're being . . . bossy."

"We can't waste time talking," Stitch responded. "Keep looking for clues."

Lilo was stunned by her friend's change in attitude.

But if Stitch was concerned, he didn't show it. He'd had it up to here with Lilo telling him he was bossy, Cobra ordering him around, and Jumba and Pleakley questioning him. Stitch remembered Cobra saying that the weird woman and the self-riding bicycle had crossed the tracks and disappeared.

So 626 knew *exactly* what he had to do.

"You stay here," Stitch said. Then he jumped onto the tracks below!

"Stitch!" Lilo shouted, her voice full of worry. "You can't just explore the tunnel on your own! We're supposed to stick together, like Cobra said! We're a team, remember?"

"Look for clues here!" Stitch yelled behind him, ignoring his friend. "That's an order!"

In a flash, Stitch went into multi-armed mode and scurried along the wall of the subway tunnel.

"Stitch, no!" Lilo hollered.

Her protests didn't register with Stitch. He knew what Cobra had said, but in his mind, that was only because no one trusted Stitch to act on his own. He was a detective, a member of the GDA, and if everyone couldn't see that, then he would show them.

"I got this," Stitch said to himself as he scrambled along the wall and out of his friends' sight.

TUNNEL CLUES

Only a couple of minutes had passed, and Lilo continued to peer down the tunnel, hoping to catch sight of Stitch.

"I'm sure he will be fine," Jumba said, trying to reassure Lilo. "Agent 626 is quite resilient. I once threw him into deep pit full of Bawk Bawks, and he came out completely unscathed."

"What's a Bawk Bawk?" Lilo asked.

"It's like a chicken," Pleakley said. "But poisonous!"

Bawk Bawk

"I don't care about Bawk Bawks," Lilo replied. "I care about Stitch! He can't just go off by himself. He's part of a team!"

"Well, he sure wasn't acting like it," Pleakley said. "He was being kind of a bossy pants if you ask me."

"No one did," Jumba said.

"You know, you could also be a little friendlier," Pleakley said. "You've been picking on me all day. Best friends are usually nicer to each other."

Jumba stuttered, like he was about to speak but didn't know what to say. Then he just waved a dismissive hand.

A frustrated Lilo said, "Will you two stop arguing? It's bad enough that Stitch decided to investigate on his own. If we're going to be a team, we need to act like one."

"I will if *he* will," Pleakley said, pointing at Jumba. "So, what do you suggest?"

"Cobra asked us to search the subway platform for clues," she said. "So that's what we should do."

"What about Stitch?" Pleakley asked.

"We'll just have to hope that he's okay and makes good decisions," Lilo said. Then, quietly, so no one else could hear, she added, "And that maybe he realizes he's being a big doo-doo head and comes back soon."

Stitch crawled along the subway tunnel ceiling. He crawled and crawled.

Then he crawled some more.

How much did he crawl, you ask? Well, on a scale of one to ten, with one being the least crawling, and ten being the most, he probably crawled about 157.

In other words, he crawled *a lot*.

And from the moment he started crawling, Stitch couldn't ignore the stink. The tunnel was full of not-so-nice odors, kind of like wet, smelly garbage. He thought about what had happened back at the platform, the way he had spoken to Jumba and Pleakley, and especially the way he had talked to Lilo. He hadn't meant to sound like that. He felt bad.

His thoughts were interrupted by a buzzing sound. Stitch jumped off the ceiling and landed on the ground. He reached into his case and pulled out the communicator. It was Lilo calling. A part of him wanted to pick up and tell Lilo he was sorry. But another part of him said to ignore the call. How could he go back to the platform and face Lilo without having accomplished *anything*? Having to admit that maybe, just maybe, she was right . . . and he was *wrong*? Well, that would mean admitting that maybe he wasn't ready to work a case by himself—to be a leader. And Stitch wasn't ready to accept that yet.

So he returned the communicator to the case without answering the call. As he was putting it inside, he saw something on the ground that looked familiar. It was a curved spike, like a long nail or . . . a tooth!

Stitch picked up the object and examined it. The thing looked almost exactly like the spike the Grand Councilwoman had shown them earlier.

He *must* be on the right path!

He started crawling along the ground. When he looked up, he noticed something different. Instead of just grubby subway tunnels, he began to see something green. Plants! There were little plants here and there, growing in cracks in the subway walls. They were unlike any plant he had ever

seen—or probably that you've ever seen. Here, take
a look:

Stitch noticed a few spray-paint cans lying on
their sides—and nearby, rats scurrying close to the
tracks and darting in and out of holes in the wall.
There were cockroaches, too, skittering back and
forth, up and down the wall, and along the ground.

The little bugs were making a distinct sound.

Click . . . Click . . . Click . . .

Reaching into his Detective Tool Belt, Stitch
rummaged around until he pulled out the
magnifying glass. He looked at one of the strange
plants for a few seconds but didn't know what else
to do with it.

Thinking he might need another detective tool, Stitch reached back into the gold case. His paw came out with a device that looked like an enormously oversized human ear. He put it over his own ear, but nothing happened. Then Stitch remembered how Cobra had spoken to the omni-compass to make it work. Maybe the ear thingy worked the same way?

"Hello, ear thingy," Stitch said. "I am—"

"Agent 626," a voice said inside the ear. "Welcome to the Intergalactic Over-Ear Translator! We can translate approximately 11,248 languages. Why not give it a try?"

In case you were wondering if the Intergalactic Over-Ear Translator really looked like an ear, check out this blueprint:

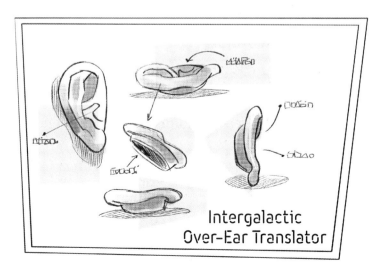

Intergalactic
Over-Ear Translator

That sparked an idea in Stitch's little furry blue head as he watched the cockroaches sitting on the subway floor, making clicking sounds.

He walked to the insects, cleared his throat, and said, "Greetings! I am Stitch!"

The answer was silence.

Stitch wondered if the Intergalactic Over-Ear Translator was broken, or maybe it didn't know how to speak "cockroach."

But a second later, Stitch heard a tiny, almost elegant voice say, "Well, hello there, darling. My, you're rather tall, aren't you? My name is Trixie."

"Hello, Trixie," Stitch replied. "I am a detective. On a case. Have you seen anything unusual?"

Trixie thought for a moment, tilting her little cockroach head to one side. "Not today, I'm afraid," she answered. "But then, I've been rather busy organizing my schedule."

Then another cockroach walked past Trixie, tapping her on the head. "What about me? You ain't asked me if I've seen somethin'!" the second cockroach said.

"Hello, Ed," Stitch said. "Have you seen anything unusual?"

"No," Ed said. "Never hurts to ask, though, am I right?"

Stitch frowned. Then he remembered the strange plants on the wall and the spray cans on the ground. "What about those?" he asked, pointing at the plants. "Have you seen these before?"

"Oh, the plants? Sure," Ed said. "Since, what, about a week ago?"

"Most assuredly, yes, a week ago," Trixie replied. "Those little plants just started popping right up all over the place, especially down there." She pointed an antenna at a small hole in the subway floor nearby.

"Yeah, I guess that's kind of unusual," Ed added. "First the bicycle, then these plants. Sheesh."

Stitch turned his head to look at Ed. "Bicycle?" he asked.

"Yeah, a bicycle. And not just any bicycle," Ed said. "It was one of those, whaddayacallit, one of them new self-riding bicycles. Right, Trixie?"

"Indeed," Trixie said. "A most luxurious model, to be sure."

A *self-riding bicycle?* Stitch wondered: Could that be the same bicycle Cobra had seen? *The bicycle and the plants must be connected somehow,* he thought. It was too much of a coincidence. Trixie and Ed had said as much. So he tapped his GDA badge, opened the Clues section, and jotted down *STRANGE PLANTS.*

Then Stitch scrambled to the hole Trixie had pointed at and looked inside. It was too dark for him to see anything, really. It was so small—maybe just big enough for him to crawl into, but he didn't see any way that a bicycle could have fit inside. The whole situation was very strange indeed.

A vibrating sound came from inside the gold case on Stitch's Detective Tool Belt. He knew it was the galactic communicator again, and he was only too aware of who was calling.

He took it out of the case.

It was Lilo.

Still not in a listening mood, Stitch simply switched off the communicator and shoved it back into the case as far as he could—as if to make it go away forever.

Then he turned his attention back to the hole.

"Thank you for your help," Stitch said to Trixie and Ed as he scampered inside the hole. He moved so quickly that he didn't notice when he dropped his Intergalactic Over-Ear Translator on the ground behind him.

"Don't mention it, darling," Trixie said.

"What, no tip?" Ed grumbled.

CHAPTER 6

Back on the subway platform, only a couple of people were waiting for the next train. Lilo stared at the galactic communicator in her hand.

"I can't believe he won't answer," she said. Stitch had disappeared over thirty minutes earlier. And while he was off doing who knew what, Lilo, Jumba, and Pleakley had been over every nook and cranny of the subway platform and turned up exactly nothing.

"You know, sometimes *friends* do things they don't mean to do," Pleakley said. "Or they act thoughtlessly."

Then he glared at Jumba, who was too busy looking at some lint he had found inside his pocket to pay attention to Pleakley.

"Or sometimes they just outright ignore their friends!" Pleakley said, fuming.

In fact, he was so angry . . .

[Hey, you—reader person—this is the part where you ask us how angry he was. Can you do that, please? Thanks!]

He was so angry that he nearly flipped his wig.

"This is awful!" Lilo said.

But before she could say anything else, there was the sound of screeching brakes as a subway train pulled into the station. The doors opened, and a crush of people flooded out of the train cars!

"Jumba! Pleakley!" Lilo called out as the people pushed past her. There were so many it seemed like she might get trampled. Take a look!

"Little girl!" Jumba shouted, and his large hand found Lilo's. The scientist scooped her off the floor and held her overhead.

The people kept on pouring out of the cars, shoving their way past Lilo and Jumba.

"Hey, find someplace else to stand!" a man wearing a fancy suit said as he pushed Pleakley aside.

"Tourists," a kid who couldn't have been much older than Lilo said as he stomped past them. The kid's mother pulled him along, and Lilo heard her say, "We'll talk about your manners when we get home."

The people kept on coming out of the train, moving toward the stairs leading out of the subway station.

At last the flow of pedestrians stopped, and the doors closed. A moment later, the train pulled out.

Jumba set Lilo back down on the floor, and the two looked around.

Lilo and Jumba were the only ones left on the platform.

"Pleakley!" Lilo yelled. "Pleakley, where are you?"
There was no answer.

Then Lilo saw it, sitting on the floor, smashed to pieces: Pleakley's galactic communicator.

"He must have been caught up in the crowd," Jumba said. "Pleakley is very light. Like feather."

"What do we do?" Lilo asked. "Without his communicator, how can we find Pleakley? And what about Stitch?"

"Is conundrum," Jumba said. "Also, terrible moment for Galactic Detective Agency to ask for update on situation."

Lilo looked at Jumba. "Why do you say that?" she asked.

"Because," Jumba said, pointing at the galactic communicator that began to vibrate in Lilo's hand, "Galactic Detective Agency is asking for update on situation."

Meanwhile—Actually, this would probably be a good time to get a snack or something, don't you think? Wouldn't a snack taste great right about now? I sure would like one. If any of you have a cordless banana, I wouldn't say no to it.

So let's get some snacks and meet back here in like five minutes, okay?

FIVE MINUTES LATER . . .

Meanwhile, again, Stitch crawled down the hole in the subway tunnel. His claws were perfect for clinging to the sides of the hole, and he was able to move quite fast. But the hole was really deep! He descended for what seemed like twenty minutes, but it was really only like three or four minutes. See, time's funny that way.

When Stitch finally emerged from the hole, he saw that he had poked his head into what looked like another, much deeper tunnel.

Letting go of the walls, Stitch dropped into the dark tunnel. Immediately, he heard a splashing sound. For a second, he almost panicked. He remembered the incident earlier that day at Turtle

Pond, when he jumped into the water, not realizing how deep it was, and instantly sunk because of his super-dense body. Luckily, there was only a couple of inches of water on the tunnel floor.

Heaving a sigh of relief, Stitch began to walk, his feet splashing along.

Looking at the tunnel walls, Stitch noticed that the concrete and metal were being overwhelmed by what looked like weird green vines of some kind. In fact, the surroundings looked less like an abandoned subway tunnel and more like a swamp.

As he kept plodding along, and the vines became more numerous, Stitch began to see strange small plants that resembled the ones he had seen in the tunnel above. That must mean he was getting closer to whatever was down there!

Stitch was so excited about his rediscovery of the weird little plants that he nearly didn't see a purple mist hovering just over the surface of the water and little bits of luminous green plant life floating along the top, almost like algae.

First the weird plants on the walls, then the purple mist, and now the glowing green algae in the water. All this was unlike the rest of the subway tunnel he had seen so far, and it struck Stitch as very odd. So he made a note of it in his Galactic Detective Agency handbook.

Then he took a step back and further analyzed the scene before him. He didn't want just to assume that the strange plants, the mist, and the glowing floating stuff were connected. That wasn't very detective-y. He needed evidence.

That seemed like another pretty good detective rule, so he made a note of it.

STITCH'S DETECTIVE RULE #13
A smart detective doesn't assume—
a smart detective collects evidence.

He thought he heard a sound ahead. Something like . . . people talking? Holding on to the vines that snaked along the walls, Stitch crawled toward the noise.

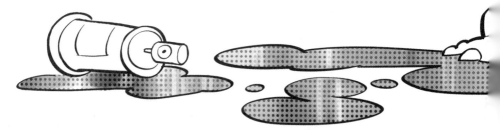

Now Stitch was *sure* that it was people talking. He made out these words:

"Going to the subway, lots of work to do.
Trek through the tunnels, beneath the avenue.
Drip-drip goes the water, as we keep on rhyming.
Watch the garden grow, isn't it enlightening?"

Stitch almost shouted, "They're rhyming!" but he covered his mouth with all his paws at once, and it looked like this:

He couldn't believe it. The Grand Councilwoman and Agent Peebles had told Stitch and his friends about the rhyming humans who had disappeared down into the subways. This must be them!

Stitch scampered forward and poked his head around the bend of the tunnel. At last he could see the people who were uttering those rhyming words. They appeared to be all different sorts of people—older, younger. Stitch noticed a young woman with large glasses, a very tall person wearing multiple gold necklaces, and a much older, surly-looking man. About the only thing they seemed to have in common was their blank, vacant stare. They all looked ahead as if in a daze and repeated the rhyme, shuffling along the murky tunnel.

Stitch noticed that each of the humans carried a spray can. The people would periodically stop walking and spritz something on the watery surface. The little cans looked familiar to him. Stitch could have sworn that he had seen them before, but he couldn't place where.

Then he remembered: when he was talking to Trixie and Ed, there had been spray cans behind the cockroaches!

(Go back and look at page 69. You'll see 'em!)

Upon closer inspection, Stitch saw that the people weren't just emitting "something" from those cans: it looked like the same purple gas that floated above the water!

Wherever the people spritzed the purple mist from their cans, Stitch saw little glowing algae emerge. And the existing vines and greenery began to flourish even more than before.

Stitch just *knew* that whatever was in those spray cans was causing this strange plant growth.

In that moment, he thought about confronting the people. But he figured he should be cautious approaching randomly rhyming people. That seemed like another important rule, so Stitch added it to his ever-growing list.

STITCH'S DETECTIVE RULE #14
Be careful about confronting weird rhyming people! You never know what they'll do.

Stitch thought about Cobra, and about how the other agent had left him behind with Lilo, Jumba, and Pleakley while *he* was going to solve the mystery all on his own. Well, now Stitch was the one who was going to crack the case, all by himself. He was sure of it!

But while he was busy being sure of it, Stitch failed to notice a soda can drift by in the murky water—a can that slowly began to change shape as it grew larger and larger, looming over Stitch.

CHAPTER 7

I'm betting after that exciting chapter, you probably forgot all about Lilo and Jumba, and that the Galactic Detective Agency was calling.

What's that? You didn't forget? Well, I did. But then, my brain is like a block of swiss cheese, and all the stuff I'm supposed to remember sneaks out of the holes.

But enough talk about cheese! Let's get back to it and pick things up right from the moment that Lilo and Jumba answered the call, shall we?

"How is the case proceeding?" the small pink alien on the other end of the signal asked.

"Before we get to that, just one question," Jumba interjected.

"Yes?" the alien said, sounding only slightly annoyed.

"Who are you again?" Jumba asked.

"Agent Peebles!" the little alien said, frustrated. "I work for the Grand Councilwoman! We've met before! Multiple times!"

"I'm sorry," Jumba said. "It's just you are very hard to remember!"

Agent Peebles muttered something unintelligible, then repeated, "How is the case proceeding?"

"It's proceeding . . . proceedingly!" Lilo said, trying to sound confident.

"Yes, 'proceedingly' . . . Well, I assume that means everything is going to plan, then," Agent Peebles replied.

Jumba nodded. "Oh, absolutely," he said. "It couldn't be going any more to plan."

"I know Agent Bubbles is investigating a situation downtown. But where is Agent 626? And Pleakley?"

Tongue-tied, Jumba stared at the hologram with

his mouth open, like an Alburian Space Camel with sixteen humps.

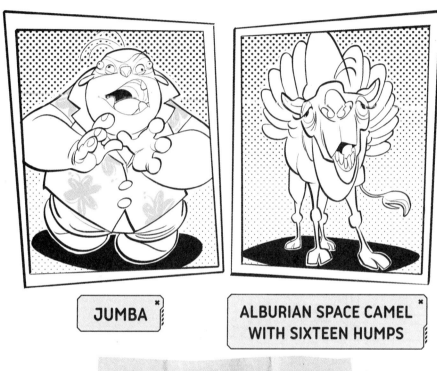

JUMBA *

ALBURIAN SPACE CAMEL *
WITH SIXTEEN HUMPS

SEE THE RESEMBLANCE?

"Stitch is investigating the tunnels, and Pleakley is, uh, securing the perimeter," Lilo said, thinking fast.

"I see! Well, it sounds like you have the situation in hand," the little pink alien said. "I'll inform the Grand Councilwoman at once."

The hologram disappeared, and Lilo let out a long sigh.

"'Securing the perimeter'?" Jumba asked.

"I had to say *something*," Lilo said. "I couldn't tell her that Stitch *and* Pleakley have disappeared. It's super not good."

"Agreed," Jumba said. "Super not good."

"And that's why we're going to do something about it," Lilo said.

"So who do we find first?" Jumba asked.

"It's obvious," Lilo said.

"Agreed," Jumba nodded. "We should go after . . ."

"Stitch is in the most danger!" Lilo shouted. "He's in that tunnel all alone! Who knows what could happen to him? Pleakley can take care of himself."

Jumba shook his head. "Are you sure? Pleakley can't even take care of a Tiberium Garden Daisy!"

"What's a Tiberium Garden Daisy?" Lilo asked.

TIBERIUM GARDEN DAISY *

"Is enormous sentient flower, capable of eating and digesting several beings all in one bite of its disgusting cavernous mouth," Jumba answered.

"I don't think *anyone* could take care of one of those!" Lilo exclaimed.

"Exactly my point!" Jumba said, seizing the moment. "Pleakley has next to no survival skills. In fact, only survival skill he has is to scream loudly at very high pitch. This is surprisingly effective in certain situations."

"You're underestimating your friend," Lilo said. "He's got more courage than you think. And he's more resourceful, too!"

"Little girl has no idea what she's talking about," Jumba said, folding his arms.

"Well, you don't, either," Lilo shot back. "I know you're worried about Pleakley. So am I. But can we go after Stitch first? Please? At least we have an *idea* where he might be. We have *no* clue where Pleakley is. And if we find Stitch, he can help us get Pleakley back."

Jumba wanted to argue some more, but deep inside, he understood what Lilo was saying, even though he couldn't bring himself to admit out loud that she was right.

"Very well," Jumba said, a little reluctantly. "You know, in your own way, you are just as persuasive as 626."

Then he lowered Lilo onto the subway tracks, following right behind her.

You might be interested to know that Pleakley once encountered a Tiberium Garden Daisy. Jumba was there, and he remembers it going something like this:

So perhaps now you see why Jumba was so
concerned about Pleakley.

Speaking of Pleakley, let's flash back to the
moment the subway train pulled into the station.
Pleakley was standing next to Jumba and Lilo.
Then came the train, and the people, and then
someone grabbed on to him!

"Hey!" Pleakley said. "Watch the hand!"

"Come with me if you want to live!" someone
said as the hand tugged at Pleakley, forcing him out
of the subway.

"I *do* want to live," Pleakley said. "I'm good at it!"

Soon they were outside, and Pleakley was finally
able to get a good look at the person who had taken

him out of the subway. It was a woman wearing a dark suit and dark glasses like Cobra's. The woman had dark hair cropped close to her head and a serious look on her face.

"What's going on here?" Pleakley demanded. "Who are you?"

"I'm Agent Zapp Weems," she said.

"Agent Zapp Weems?" Pleakley said as they made it to the corner of Forty-Second Street and Fifth Avenue. "Is that a made-up name? Like an alias?"

"That's need-to-know information," Zapp said. "And you don't need to know. Anyway. We got word from the Galactic Detective Agency that aliens were going to try to kidnap you, Pleakley."

"Kidnap me?" Pleakley exclaimed. "Who would want to kidnap *me*?"

"It's a long list," Zapp replied. "But if you must know, there's a group of evil alien scientists that wants to use your knowledge of the humans' mosquito population for sinister purposes."

"My mosquito knowledge?" Pleakley said, horrified. "For sinister purposes? Why, the idea is simply terrifying!"

"Exactly," Zapp said. "The Grand Councilwoman ordered me to track you down and take you into protective custody. Luckily, you just happened to be standing there when I got out of that subway car. I used the cover of that crowd to whisk you away to safety."

"But what about my friends? Lilo! Jumba! And

Stitch! We need to contact them immediately!"
Pleakley said.

"That's a big no-can-do," Zapp replied. "Too
risky. Don't worry about your friends. They'll be
fine. The threat we received was against you, and
you only. You're my mission, Pleakley."

"Wow," Pleakley said. "I've never been anyone's
mission before."

"First time for everything," Zapp said. "But now
we need to get you to our safe house. I've got a ferry
waiting to take us—"

"That sounds great," Pleakley said. "But first
can't we do a little sightseeing? I mean, I've come all
the way to New York, and I've got this book—"

"That wouldn't be safe," Zapp said, tugging at Pleakley's hand.

"Just one little touristy thing," Pleakley begged. "Please? Pretty please? I promise we can go after that."

Zapp glared at Pleakley, then rolled her eyes. "Oh, all right. But just the one!"

CHAPTER 8

THE TOOTHOIDS

As Stitch observed the weird rhyming people spraying purple mist on the glowing algae and plants in the abandoned subway tunnel, he gradually became aware of a sound coming from behind him.

Was it . . . growling?

When he swiveled his head to the left to look, Stitch saw it.

The snarling soda can was looming over him!

Only it was looking less and less like a soda can

by the second as it grew larger and bulkier. Eyes appeared, glaring, staring, burning with evil!

A moment later, the "soda can" was no more. In its place stood a large dog-sized creature that looked like some kind of cross between an alligator and a rat! The thing had an absolutely ginormous mouth full of absolutely ginormous teeth! It screeched loudly, baring its teeth right in 626's face!

Stitch jumped back, putting some much-needed distance between him and the creature.

Maybe he should have been afraid, facing this dangerous moment all on his own. But Stitch wasn't afraid. In fact, he was feeling excited! On a scale of one to ten, with one being the least excited and ten being the most, Stitch was a . . .

Forty-two is more than ten!

Excited as Stitch was, the detective in him told him to think. Before he could do anything about the creature, he needed to know what it was and if it had any weaknesses. Then Stitch remembered that Cobra had told him about the GLURBs, the glasses that could help him identify different aliens. Stitch reached into the gold case on his Detective Tool Belt and fumbled around until he found the glasses and put them on.

But nothing happened.

Then he remembered that Cobra had said something about having to activate the glasses' "Scan for Alien" feature . . . and that Jumba and Pleakley had been talking too loud for Stitch to hear it.

This book blames us for EVERYTHING.

The creature swiped its tail at Stitch, and he jumped to one side, barely avoiding the strike. Stitch landed on the watery ground and rolled. The thing leaped at Stitch, and he kept on rolling, narrowly escaping his attacker.

This wasn't getting him anywhere. Stitch needed to turn the glasses on, but he didn't know how.

But he knew someone who did.

Lilo.

She had listened and heard what Cobra was saying. But Lilo wasn't there right now—because Stitch hadn't wanted her to be there. Because he had wanted to prove he could do everything by himself.

The creature thrashed its tail at Stitch, hitting him in the belly and knocking him into a wall right behind the weird rhyming people. They didn't even notice. As if in a trance, they just kept rhyming and spraying the algae.

"Ow!" Stitch groaned as he quickly got to his feet. There was no time to think about what had happened or any regrets he might have. He had to figure out how to work the glasses—and fast.

That was when it hit him. Stitch had been so

busy trying to evade the beast and getting knocked around that he hadn't been able to really think! He recalled that Cobra had activated the omni-compass by talking to it, and the Intergalactic Over-Ear Translator had worked the same way. What if turning on the "Scan for Alien" feature was as simple as saying—

Scan for alien!

To his relief, the GLURBs spoke, replying, "Scanning now."

Almost immediately, a heads-up message on the glasses announced, **_ALIEN IDENTIFIED_**.

Then Stitch saw this file appear on the GLURBs' heads-up display:

WARNING!

**TOOTHOIDS MAY BE ABLE TO CHANGE SHAPE—
TO BECOME ANYONE OR ANYTHING.**

Excessive rotation produces extreme nausea.

"Toothoids!" Stitch exclaimed.

At once things began to make sense. The "soda can" had been a disguised Toothoid. If they could truly change shape and become anything, then maybe the bicycle and the garbage cans Cobra had gone to investigate were all Toothoids, too.

Speaking of which, two more Toothoids appeared from a crack in the tunnel wall to join the original creature, and together the trio of terrors advanced on Stitch.

"You cannot be allowed to leave here knowing who we are!" one of the Toothoids said, showing off its mouthful of jagged teeth.

Stitch considered that for a moment. But he realized that even though he was in incredible danger, he had actually completed the first objective from the Grand Councilwoman's assignment!

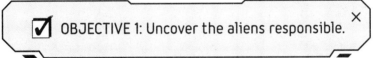

"Stitch did it!" he shouted.

But just as he finished congratulating himself, the Toothoids attacked.

Their tails lashed out, extending like uncoiling springs. Long and slender like a rat's tail but covered in a thick, scaly hide like an alligator's, the Toothoids' appendages struck Stitch.

CHAPTER 9

How long have you been reading this book now? A half hour? An hour? Two hours? Days?! You probably need a break—maybe go and stretch your legs, pet a dog or something, right?

Well, go ahead and do that. This book isn't going anywhere.

Unless it's secretly a Toothoid.

(It's not, don't worry . . . maybe.)

Anyway, while Stitch confronted the new alien threat, Lilo and Jumba traipsed down the subway tunnel in search of their blue-furred friend.

"Stay close to me, Jumba," Lilo said. "You never know what we're going to find."

"I know what we're *not* going to find," Jumba snapped. "Pleakley. We should be searching for him instead of stomping through subway tunnel."

"But you said it was okay to—" Lilo protested.

"I never said was okay," Jumba grumbled. "Only that I would go along with it. Is mistake. Big mistake. Little girl thinks she knows everything."

"I think I know everything?" Lilo exploded. "What about you? *You're* the one who's supposed to be a genius scientist!"

"'Supposed to be'?" Jumba roared. "What does that mean?"

"If you were so smart, you could have figured out a way to, I don't know, track Stitch *or* Pleakley! And instead we don't know where either one of them is, and you're no help! All you do is complain!" Lilo said.

"All I do is complain? Well, all you do is whine and criticize my genius!"

Lilo glared at Jumba.

There was silence as they stood there in the tunnel, fuming at each other.

And then, finally, Jumba said, "We—"

"*We* aren't talking!" Lilo shot back, cutting him off.

"No," Jumba persisted. "We are being *watched*."

Then he tapped Lilo on the shoulder with a huge finger.

Lilo turned around and saw that Jumba was pointing at a pair of cockroaches sitting next to his right foot.

"What are those?" Jumba said. "They've been following us whole time."

"Those are cockroaches," Lilo replied. "I wonder why they're staring at us."

"I'm sure there is perfectly logical explanation," Jumba said.

Then there was a tiny sound.

Click . . . Click . . . Click . . .

Lilo noticed that it came from the cockroaches.

"I think they're trying to say something," Lilo said.

"Ha! Ridiculous!" Jumba laughed.

Then one of the cockroaches skittered away. A few seconds later it returned, dragging what looked like a huge ear.

"What is cockroach doing with Intergalactic Over-Ear Translator?" Jumba said.

"You know what it is?" Lilo asked.

"Of course I know what it is. I took credit for inventing it! You simply put it over your ear and—"

Before Jumba could finish, Lilo had already put on the translator. Jumba leaned over, pulled a small earplug on a cord from the center of the translator, and put it in his ear.

"Prepare to be disappointed," Jumba said. "I am telling you, there is no way these so-called cockroaches can ta—"

"Hey! You! The big fella with the know-it-all attitude! Take it down a notch!"

The voice came from one of the cockroaches.

Lilo shot Jumba a *See? I TOLD you so* look, and Jumba shrugged.

"Yes!" Lilo exclaimed. "You can talk! My name is Lilo, and I'm looking for my friend Stitch. He's a little furry blue guy. Have you seen him?"

"Oh, without question," one of the cockroaches said. "I'm Trixie, by the by. A pleasure to make your acquaintance. And this fellow is Ed."

"Nice to meet you, Trixie and Ed!" Lilo said as she kneeled down next to the cockroaches. "You're really polite."

"Well, manners *are* important," Trixie replied. "Anyway, your little blue friend, he went thataway."

Trixie pointed at a small hole in the subway floor. "Your friend went down that hole. Right in, quick as you please."

"Do you know why he went in there?" Lilo asked.

"As a matter of fact, I do," Trixie replied. "A couple days ago, I saw a bicycle ride itself down this very tunnel and go down that hole."

Jumba's eyes widened. "How does big bicycle fit in tiny hole?" he wondered.

"It sure was weird," Trixie agreed. "Not something you see every day. And I'm a cockroach that lives in New York City, so that's saying something."

"We have to go down that hole," Lilo said. "Wherever Stitch went, that's where we're going."

"But how?" Jumba asked, pointing at the small hole. "You go in hole? You are tiny, no problem. Me? I am great big scientist—so big probably because I am mostly brains, and as everyone knows, brains take up most space."

Jumba   **Jumba's Brain**

Lilo looked at the hole again and thought of Stitch, all alone. Maybe she should go after him by herself? But then she thought about Jumba. She couldn't just leave him, even if she was mad at him. They were a team. And teams, like families, stuck together.

"Well, we just need to make the hole bigger!" Lilo said. "Do you have any gadget that could help with that?"

"Gadgets? Me? No," Ed the cockroach said,

shaking his head. "Sorry. But—and I don't wanna brag or nothin'—I *do* have an extensive collection of bottle caps."

"I think little girl was talking to me," Jumba replied. "Let me see."

Fumbling through his pockets, Jumba took out a long piece of string, some lint, and a spoon.

"What about that?" Lilo asked, pointing to the spoon. "Can we dig the hole bigger?"

"I suppose we could," Jumba said. "But then what will I use to eat my cereal? Breakfast is most important meal of day."

"I'll get you a new one," Lilo said. "Now let's dig!"

As Lilo and Jumba began the task of making a very big hole with a very small spoon, Trixie and Ed sat and watched.

"Ed, darling," Trixie said, "are you thinking what I'm thinking?"

"I dunno," Ed said, shrugging. "It all depends what yer thinkin'."

"Well, dearest, I'm thinking that it would be absolutely splendid to tag along with those two, eh?

Get out of our little tunnel, see something of the world. What say you?"

"Sounds good to me!" Ed said, scratching his head. "Let's follow 'em!"

CHAPTER 10

CONFIDENTIAL

ICE CREAM

CONFIDENTIAL

While Lilo and Jumba worked on widening the hole, Stitch faced an entirely different obstacle down below.

He steadied himself in the subway tunnel, bracing his body against a curved vine-covered wall. Looking behind him, he saw the three Toothoids coming closer, their mouths open, sharp teeth bared.

"This one might alert others to our presence. He must not be allowed to leave," one of the Toothoids snarled. The fearsome creature turned to the weird rhyming humans and shouted, "Get him—now!"

As Stitch moved farther down the tunnel, he heard the chants of the rhyming humans grow louder. Looking up, he saw the group of them now staggering toward him, arms extended like they were some kind of sleepwalking zombies.

Stitch darted toward the nearest human. It was a surly-looking older man whose eyes were open wide as could be.

"Hey! Mister!" Stitch said as he shook the surly man by the waist. "Yoo-hoo! Wakey wakey!"

But the surly man didn't "wakey wakey."

The Toothoids advanced one claw-footed step at a time.

Stitch did everything he could think of to get the man's attention:

But nothing he did seemed to break the man's concentration. Then Stitch realized it wasn't concentration. The man had been *hypnotized*. And it didn't take a detective to realize that the ones who had hypnotized him were the Toothoids.

So Stitch had pieced together more of the case but was now faced with a trio of terrifying Toothoids and their army of zombified humans!

With his incredibly strong legs, Stitch propelled himself into the tunnel, putting some distance between him and his fanged pursuers. He landed in the algae-filled water.

SPLASH!

Stitch ran ahead on all his limbs. The growling of Toothoids and the sound of the hypnotized rhyming humans followed close behind:

"Going to the subway, lots of work to do.
Trek through the tunnels, beneath the avenue.
Drip-drip goes the water, as we keep on rhyming.
Watch the garden grow, isn't it enlightening?"

It was in that moment that Stitch began to experience something he had never felt before. It started as a slight queasiness in his stomach, and it seemed to travel all the way up to his brain. Maybe . . . maybe he was in over his head. He wanted to prove that he could be a really good detective all on his own. But now there was so much going on!

There were the hypnotized humans, and there were the strange happenings in the subway tunnel with the purple gas and all the plants. And on top of that, there were angry Toothoids chasing him. Sure, he could solve any one of those problems by himself. But solving all three? At the same time? If only Lilo were there, and even Jumba and Pleakley, they might be able to come up with a plan together, to figure a way out of this mess.

And then Stitch heard a little voice inside his head.

"Don't give up!" the voice said. "You're Experiment 626! You can do anything!"

That seemed like a pretty amazing detective rule to Stitch, so he made a note to add it later:

STITCH'S DETECTIVE RULE #15

Never give up—that's your superpower!

Then, with a burst of energy, he whirled around, raised his hands, and growled at the oncoming Toothoids and shambling, hypnotized humans.

He decided that keeping the Toothoids off balance might buy him some time, so he did the thing he hoped the aliens would least expect. He charged right at them, and it looked like this:

"This ice cream is delicious!" Pleakley exclaimed as he at last stood on the eighty-sixth floor observation deck atop the Empire State Building, licking an ice-cream cone. Agent Weems stood next to him, a scowl on her face. While Stitch and his friends were exploring the subway tunnels, Pleakley had spent nearly an hour deciding where he wanted to go from his New York travel guide before finally settling on the Empire State Building. "Say, what do you call this flavor?"

"Vanilla," Agent Weems replied.

"Vanilla is amazing!" Pleakley said.

Pleakley and Agent Weems were the only ones on the deck.

"Tell me, how did you get them to clear the entire area just for us?" Pleakley asked.

"I, uh, told them that you were the, ah, president in disguise," Agent Weems replied.

"Really? Wow," Pleakley said, sounding pleased. "President of what?"

Agent Weems shook her head as Pleakley continued eating his ice cream.

"This is great, but I can't help feeling guilty,

standing here with you, taking in the amazing view of New York City, and eating delicious vanilla ice cream while my friends might be in terrible jeopardy!" Pleakley said.

Agent Weems waved her hand. "Like I said, your friends are just fine," she said. "They're right where we want them."

"How's that again?" Pleakley asked.

"They're safe, that's what I mean," Agent Weems replied. "Just like you."

Pleakley nodded, and he took another lick of his ice-cream cone. "It feels good to be safe. And this view is incredible! Breathtaking. And I can't wait to go somewhere else. Like a hot-dog cart! Have you ever been to a hot-dog cart?!"

Agent Weems bit her lower lip. "No, I haven't," she said through gritted teeth.

"Neither have I, but if I remember the guidebook— the one you took from me that you won't give back—well, the guidebook says hot dogs from a New York City hot-dog cart are the best hot dogs in the world. *The world!* Can you imagine?"

Agent Weems looked like she'd had just about

enough of Pleakley's babbling, when she pointed toward one side of the observation deck and shouted, "Look! A giant ape is climbing that building!"

"Where?" Pleakley shouted as he ran across the deck, dropping his ice-cream cone.

POSSIBLY THE SADDEST MOMENT IN THIS BOOK

While Pleakley looked over the edge of the building, trying to get a glimpse of the gigantic climbing ape, Agent Weems crept up behind him with her arms extended—like she was going to push Pleakley over the edge!

But just as it appeared that she would shove the

unaware alien, Pleakley took a step to the left and said, "Agent Weems, I don't see an ape anywhere!"

Unfortunately for Agent Weems, she was moving too fast. She tried to stop but slipped on the ice cream Pleakley had dropped only moments before. Her momentum took her right through one of the holes in the protective grate as she accidentally hurled herself over the side of the Empire State Building!

As Pleakley raced to the other side of the observation deck in his quest to see the giant ape, Agent Weems quickly morphed into a small bird. Then she flew back to the observation deck and morphed back into her guise as Agent Weems.

AGENT WEEMS
IS A TOOTHOID!!!

"I can't believe this," Pleakley said. "There's no sign of any giant ape anywhere!"

"Yes," Agent Weems grumbled at the one-eyed alien. "*That's* the thing I can't believe."

"It only makes sense, though," Pleakley said, unaware of everything that had just happened. "I mean, the only scientist brilliant enough to engineer something like a gigantic building-climbing ape is Jumba, and he hasn't done it. Yet."

Pleakley smiled at Agent Weems.

She forced herself to smile back as she muttered under her breath, "Next time, you get the vaporizer."

"What was that?" Pleakley asked.

"Nothing!" Agent Weems said. "Nothing. Just . . . can we go now?"

"Absolutely!" Pleakley announced brightly. "Let's go find a hot-dog cart!"

CHAPTER 11

You know what this book could use? A good rhyme!

Unfortunately, we don't have one. All we've got is this little ditty:

"Going to the subway, lots of work to do.

Trek through the tunnels, beneath the avenue.

Drip-drip goes the water, as we keep on rhyming.

Watch the garden grow, isn't it enlightening?"

Which must mean that it's time to get back to what Stitch is up to. When we last saw our blue-furred friend, he was turning the tables on the Toothoids, charging right for them!

The aliens and their captives had finally encircled Stitch, who stood there, motionless.

The Toothoids laughed.

"So this is the 'great' Agent 626," one of them said in an extremely high-pitched voice.

"Yes, that's right," said another Toothoid in a very deep voice. "We *know* who you are."

The Toothoids and their army of hypnotized humans took a step forward, drawing nearer to Stitch.

"Your capture was far easier than anticipated," said a Toothoid with a voice that was neither high nor deep, but somewhere in between. The creature then reached into his mouth and pulled out a small green metallic box covered in Toothoid drool.

"We were led to believe that you were a fierce fighter, capable of much destruction," the Toothoid with the green box continued. "I guess the stories about your vaunted prowess were exactly that . . . stories."

"And now you have fallen victim to Myron, Barry, and Zoey!" the Toothoid with the high-pitched voice cheered. "I'm Myron, by the way. That's Barry, and that's Zoey. Barry, contact the Exalted One! Let them know who we have captured today!"

"Whom," Barry, the deep-voiced Toothoid, replied.

"What?" Myron asked.

"It's supposed to be 'Let them know *whom* we have captured today.'"

"Is it? What did I say?" Myron said.

"'Who,'" Zoey chimed in.

"Wow, I will never get the hang of words," Myron said. "Anyway, let them know while I use the H.A.H.A.* to hypnotize our little 'friend'!"

Myron took the small green metallic box

* Hypnotic Autonomic Hypnosis Apparatus. This book sure loves acronyms.

from Barry and showed it to Stitch. *H.A.H.A.* was emblazoned on it. "You see, Agent 626, this small box is capable of great things! It hypnotizes its targets, reducing them to mindless servants who will do our bidding!"

"Myron," Barry said, interrupting, "why are you telling him that? Isn't that supposed to be a secret?"

"Whoops," Myron said, putting a hand to his mouth. "My bad. Anyway, I thought I told you to call the Exalted One! Do that while I hypnotize 626!"

Just as Barry was about to contact the Exalted One over the comms system, Myron approached Stitch with the H.A.H.A. pointed right at him. From behind, Zoey grabbed Stitch.

Except . . . it wasn't Stitch!

"This . . . this can't be right," Myron said. "This is not Agent 626. This is just plant goop!"

"Perhaps he is made of plant goop?" Zoey mused.

But no, Stitch was not made of plant goop. Only his hastily constructed *dummy* was made of plant goop!

And at that moment, Myron felt a fingernail gently tapping on his shoulder. The Toothoid turned around only to see Stitch—the *real* Stitch—smiling broadly and waving his paw.

The creature dropped the H.A.H.A., and in an instant, Stitch was on his paws. He hit the tunnel floor, muck splashing everywhere. With the stomp of an incredibly dense foot, Stitch completely and totally on purpose smashed the H.A.H.A. device to pieces.

"He must be super dense!" Myron shouted. "Only super-dense things can shatter the rare metal used to make the H.A.H.A.!"

"Again, that is too much information, Myron!" Barry yelled.

"My bad!" Myron hollered.

Stitch wasted no time. He darted through Myron's legs as the Toothoid tried to grab him. Stitch was far too fast, and the alien missed.

Undeterred, the Toothoids scurried along the ground, racing after Stitch.

"Hey! He broke our thingy that we really needed! Get him!" Myron shouted. "Get him a lot!" The Toothoids were tenacious. Everywhere Stitch scrambled, no matter which way he turned, there was a Toothoid right behind him. They seemed to be almost as fast as him.

But as Stitch dodged and avoided the attack of the Toothoids, he noticed something strange happening in the background. The rhyming chant was slowing down!

"Going to the . . . subway?" he heard the humans chanting in unison. "Lots of . . . work to . . . do?"

Stitch was wondering what was going on, when, swiftly, Myron swiped his long, scaly tail at the blue alien.

The tail swipe sent Stitch flying into a vine-covered wall, and he landed with a dull thud. "That hurts!" he shouted.

As he recovered from the Toothoid's attack, Stitch saw that the hypnotized humans no longer appeared to be staring blankly ahead. They were blinking and talking—and not in rhyme, either! "What the heck am I doing here?" a surly-looking man said. "Where's Ms. Muggins?"

"Last thing I remember was seeing a weird bicycle riding all by itself," a businesswoman said. "Now I'm in a subway tunnel? Gross!"

By then almost everyone in the group of hypnotized humans seemed to be shaking themselves out of the trance.

Then a short woman wearing very thick glasses turned to look directly at Stitch. She seemed completely normal!

"Hey, kid!" the woman shouted at Stitch. "Yeah, I'm talkin' to you. Are those your alligators?"

She pointed at the Toothoids.

"Alligators in the sewer," an older man wearing

a hat with a cartoon dog on it said. "This city has gone to the dogs."

He proceeded to walk down the tunnel as the other un-hypnotized humans followed him.

"Hey!" Myron called after the exiting humans. "Come back here! This . . . this isn't optional! We need you!"

Torn between corralling the departing people— and finding some way to re-hypnotize them— and capturing Agent 626, the Toothoids made their choice. The three fearsome fanged creatures descended upon Stitch all at once, their tails swiping. Wherever Stitch jumped, the tails followed, smashing.

Each swipe missed him, but only by a little. Stitch was tired and starting to slow down. He couldn't keep up the pace forever. And with each new attack, the Toothoids were coming closer to hurting him.

Stitch knew that if he couldn't stop the Toothoids on his own, he had to find a way out. The Toothoids didn't seem to tire, and their attacks were relentless.

Then a tail swept into Stitch's chest and knocked the wind out of him.

Meanwhile, two tiny creatures had their eyes on Stitch.

Stitch had to do something to stop the Toothoids . . . but what? And how?

Then he heard someone scream, "You leave Stitch alone!"

CHAPTER 12

Stitch whirled around at the sound of the voice he recognized only too well. There was Lilo with Jumba, standing in the wet vine-covered subway tunnel with their fists raised, ready for a fight!

"Lilo!" Stitch yelled, his heart swelling. "And also, Jumba!"

"'Also Jumba'?" the scientist said, sounding offended. "I have come to rescue and all I get is 'Also Jumba'?"

"But where is Pleakley?" Stitch asked.

"Is long story," Jumba said.

Stitch couldn't believe that his friends had found him. Seeing them there, coming to his aid, just when he didn't know what else to do . . . Stitch didn't have words for how good that felt.

But there was no time for Stitch to dwell on that. Lilo had already taken off in pursuit of the three Toothoids. Stitch, who had been running *from* the Toothoids, now changed direction. We would describe what he did next, but it's actually cooler if you see it for yourself.

As Myron sailed past Lilo and Jumba, the remaining Toothoids, Barry and Zoey*, sprang up behind the duo. But Jumba surprised Lilo when he turned around and snatched up the Toothoids, one in each hand.

"Aha!" Jumba said. "Unexpected, no?"

"Very unexpected!" Lilo replied. "But very cool!"

* With a *Z.*

Jumba grinned as the Toothoids tried to take a swing at him. But their arms were so tiny in comparison to their own bodies, let alone Jumba, they couldn't begin to reach him.

"Why don't you pick on someone your own size!" Barry cried.

"How about you don't pick on anyone at all?" Lilo shot back.

Oh, I do like her. She's got spirit.

An' she's right! That creep's a total bully!

That only seemed to further enrage the Toothoids, and they poised to swing their mighty tails at Jumba. But try as they might, they couldn't make their tails budge. Their eyes rotated around in their sockets, looking behind them, until they saw the reason.

At once, Barry and Zoey panicked. Their bodies began to morph in an effort to wriggle free from Stitch's iron grasp. Jumba was still holding on to them, too. Just not as iron-y.

First they tried morphing into Earth things, like humans, bicycles, garbage cans, and turtles. But every time they changed, Stitch and Jumba held fast. There was no way they were going to let go!

So then the Toothoids started to transform into some not-Earth things. Those included:

TRIMERIAN
BLOOP BEAST *

FOUR-FOOTED *
ZOOGLITH

CAT *

140

But it didn't make a difference. Whatever they turned into, no matter how much they squirmed, the Toothoids were trapped.

As the aliens struggled, Stitch faced Lilo and Jumba. Together, they had captured the Toothoids.

Together.

And that was when it dawned on Stitch that maybe being a leader wasn't all about shouting orders and telling people what to do.

"Stitch is sorry," he said. "I wanted to prove I could be leader, but we are a team. We work together."

"It's *'ohana*," Lilo replied. "*'Ohana* means—"

"Family," Jumba said. "Family means nobody gets left behind or forgotten."

Amazed, Lilo stared at Jumba.

What are you staring at? I pay attention!

"After taking down those Toothoids, I think we need a group hug," Lilo said.

"Afraid group hug will have to wait," Jumba said, scanning the tunnel. "Did anyone else notice that one Toothoid escaped?"

CHAPTER 13

As it turned out, Jumba was the first at the time to recognize that Myron was no longer in the sewer tunnel.

Stitch thought that Myron might be there still but disguised as something else. Maybe he was a vine? Or a soda can? Stitch reached into the Detective Tool Belt to find his GLURBs so he could activate the "Scan for Alien" feature.

But to his shock, the GLURBs weren't in there. Stitch realized that sometime during the confrontation with the Toothoids, he must have dropped the glasses.

Without the GLURBs to help, Stitch figured the next best thing he could do was share with Lilo and Jumba the clues he had discovered so far. Lilo and Jumba told Stitch all about Pleakley and how he had vanished in the crowd back at the subway station, leaving his communicator behind.

"Um . . . excuse me . . ." someone said behind them.

Stitch looked over his shoulder and saw the two captured Toothoids.

"Hello. Over here, Toothoid talking," Barry said. "It's great that you guys are catching up or whatever, but you know we're still here, right?"

"Yes! We are! And we could cause trouble at a moment's notice!" Zoey added.

"No, you can't!" Stitch said. "We foiled your plans!"

"Oh, yeah?" Zoey sneered. "You don't even *know* our plans."

"Yet," Stitch said, correcting the Toothoid.

"Huh?" Barry said.

Lilo walked over to Barry and Zoey, getting right into their faces.

"You're gonna spill the beans," Lilo said with a smile on her face.

"But we have no beans to spill!" Barry said. "We don't even know what beans are!"

"'Spill the beans' means you are going to tell us everything," Lilo explained.

"Never!" Barry said.

Stitch stared at the Toothoids and remembered something he had seen in their file. Something about excessive rotation causing extreme nausea.

"How about we go for a spin?" Stitch asked.

"No," Barry said. "Oh, no."

Swiftly, Stitch whipped both Toothoids around his head by their tails, swinging them in circles over and over again until the Toothoids became a blur.

The color on their faces changed to a sickly blue, and both Toothoids looked like they were about to—how shall we put this—*hurl*.

"We give!" Barry shouted.

"Yes!" Zoey yelled. "Just make it stop! I'm going to lose my lunch! And breakfast! And last night's dinner! And—"

"Okay, okay, we get it," Jumba said.

Stitch stopped whipping the dizzy, sick-looking Toothoids around and set them down on the subway floor. As the color came back to the aliens' faces, they staggered around, bumping into each other.

"We'll tell you whatever you want to know," Zoey said. "Just please don't do that again. My seven stomachs are still spinning!"

Stitch smiled. He pulled up the list of clues he had been assembling.

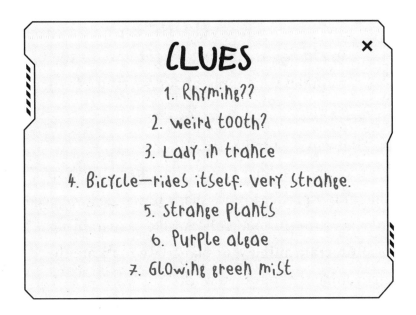

CLUES ✕
1. Rhyming??
2. weird tooth?
3. Lady in trance
4. Bicycle—rides itself. very strange.
5. strange plants
6. Purple algae
7. Glowing green mist

"Let's start with plants," Stitch said, gesturing to the vine-covered walls of the subway tunnel and the purple mist floating above the water.

"This?" Barry said. "This is nothing. It's just the beginning. We are in the process of terraforming your Earth."

"Terraforming?" Lilo asked.

Stitch activated the *GDA Official Handbook*, then opened the encyclopedia contained within it. A hologram of the entry appeared before them.

> **TERRAFORM**
>
> To change the environment of a place to make it capable of supporting life. ✕

"But why?" Stitch asked.

Zoey splashed her foot in the water. "It's simple," she said. "In order for our plans to succeed, we need to make sure this planet is capable of sustaining us. By terraforming your planet, we replicate the environment of our own world."

"That is why you see all the vines and glowing vegetation," Barry added. "It's just like our home! We used this subway tunnel as our testing ground to see if it would work. And it has, with spectacular results!"

"You call bunch of plants in subway tunnel 'spectacular'?" Jumba said.

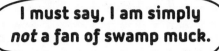

I must say, I am simply *not* a fan of swamp muck.

You can say that again!

"Look, we all have to start somewhere," Zoey shot back.

"But what is purple gas?" Stitch asked.

"A growth formula," Barry explained. "It primed the plants, so to speak. Made them more receptive to the rhymes."

"The rhymes," Lilo gasped. "That's why you needed people!"

Barry sighed. "We hypnotized the humans into working for us so we could terraform your planet faster. The rhyming causes the humans to keep talking, over and over and over. And the near-constant talking caused accelerated plant growth with the help of the purple mist."

Lilo's eyes widened. "That's because talking to plants can help them grow!"

"Exactly," Zoey said. "Wow, you're pretty smart."

Lilo smiled.

"I also am smart," Jumba said.

"Yeah, well, *she's* the one who figured it out," Zoey said, jabbing him.

"So . . . humans hypnotized, rhyme and talk, plants grow," Stitch said, wrapping his head around the Toothoids' plot. "But why not hypnotize Stitch?"

"Excellent question," Barry said, shaking his head. "I think it might have something to do with the fact that you broke the H.A.H.A. before we could use it on you."

Zoey nodded.

"But that doesn't explain why you terraformed just this subway tunnel," Lilo said.

"Not just the subway," Barry said. "Your entire planet! That's how we were going to pave the way for the big invasion."

"Big invasion?" Stitch asked. "Tell us about invasion!"

"Whoa there, little fella!" Zoey said. "We don't know anything more than that. We're just minions. Grunts. Myron was the one in charge. He knows but doesn't tell us everything."

"Yes, like about the whole 'UHOP' thing," Barry interjected. "I heard Myron mention it once, but then he dropped it—never brought it up again."

The name UHOP sounded familiar to Stitch. He could have sworn that he had heard it before, but he couldn't remember where or when. So he made a notation in his *GDA Official Handbook*.

OBJECTIVE 1: Uncover the aliens responsible.

OBJECTIVE 2: Find out the aliens' plans.

OBJECTIVE 3: Put a stop to the aliens' plans.

UHOP???
Find out more!

"Is certainly strange," Jumba said, rubbing his chin. "Sounds like Snailiens' plan. But why two alien species try to take over Earth so close to each other?"

"That's definitely weird," Lilo said.

Stitch thought about that for a moment and wondered. Could the Toothoids' plans somehow be connected to what the Snailiens had tried to do in France?

"We should get back to the surface and contact Cobra and the GDA," Lilo said.

"Yes, tell what's-their-name what is going on," Jumba added. "In meantime, what do we do about these two?"

Stitch reached into the Detective Tool Belt and

brought out what looked like a tiny yellow cage. He set it on the ground, and a moment later, the object grew, completely engulfing the two Toothoids.

"That should hold you until the GDA comes to get you," Lilo said.

The Toothoids looked at the bars that held them, sighed, and said in unison, "This is fine."

Then Barry looked at Jumba and said, "Oh, and give our regards to that Pleakley fella."

"Wait," Jumba replied. "You know Pleakley?"

"Sure, we know him," Zoey answered. "We know all about the Earth mosquito expert! That guy's in a world of trouble. Our plan was to separate you, and he was the easiest target."

"But how did you know where we would be?" Lilo asked.

Barry looked at Jumba and said, "Let me know if this looks familiar."

A moment later, Barry morphed into a small turtle.

"Is turtle!" Jumba exclaimed. "Same turtle that bonked its little head against my colossal foot back at Turtle Pond!"

The turtle shifted shape, becoming Barry again. "Exactly. We had followed Agent Bubbles to Central Park. We knew where you'd be going right from the start. Anyway, Pleakley's in our custody now. Myron is probably on his way to get him."

"What will Myron do with him?" Lilo asked.

Zoey shrugged. "He'll probably just vaporize him into total nothingness," she said. "You know, the usual."

"Vaporize him?" Stitch exclaimed. "No one vaporizes Pleakley!"

He almost started to run down the tunnel, back toward the hole through which he had entered, so that he could go and find Pleakley on his own.

But he stopped himself.

"Stitch wants to be great detective," he said, facing Lilo and Jumba, "and save Pleakley. But he can't do everything by himself. Not anymore. Stitch needs your help. We do this together."

Lilo smiled at her friend and gave Stitch a big hug. "Together," she said.

"Together!" Jumba shouted as he wrapped both Lilo and Stitch up in an enormous bear hug. "Now tell us where to find Pleakley!"

"Yes," Stitch insisted. "Give us coordinates, and maybe Grand Councilwoman won't send you to Noodelon Six!"

"Not Noodelon Six, the sixth-worst noodle planet!" Barry gasped. "It's even worse than Noodelon Five, the fifth-worst noodle planet!"

"Yes, it is one worse! That may not seem like a lot, but it makes a huge, horrible difference!" Zoey said.

"We'll tell you, we'll tell you!" Barry added.

And a moment later, Stitch and his friends had the coordinates and took off in pursuit of Pleakley.

CHAPTER 14

CONFIDENTIAL

ICE CREAM CRAVINGS

CONFIDENTIAL

"What a marvelous boat!" Pleakley exclaimed.

He stood on the deck of a small futuristic-looking ship. It was sort of a cross between a ferry and the spaceship Stitch had once stolen from the Galactic Federation, back when he escaped from their custody and flew to Earth. It had a sleek rounded design, with no sharp corners, and sported what looked like an enormous fan-driven engine.

"And what a view!" Pleakley continued. He was looking out over the Hudson River at the New Jersey coast. To the south, he could see a small island and a large green statue of a woman holding a torch to the sky.

"That's the Statue of Liberty!" he said to a less-than-enthused Agent Weems, who was standing beside him. "Did you know that some Galactic Federation scientists *still* think the Statue of Liberty is made of marshmallows? I mean, if it was, how could it stand up? Anyway, if they had just read the guidebook that you snatched away from me—which I'm still a little upset about if I'm being honest—they would know different."

"Fascinating," Agent Weems said with a roll of her eyes behind her dark glasses. She had told the unsuspecting alien that this "ferry" was issued by the Galactic Federation, which in a sense was true: Agent Weems had stolen it from them. It was a spaceship that could transform into a watercraft.

She had tried to be patient as Pleakley dragged her around the city on his whirlwind tour. At each opportunity, Agent Weems had attempted to eliminate Pleakley. And at each turn, she had failed.

This was great for Pleakley but less great—and more painful—for Agent Weems.

Take a look and you'll see what we mean.

"Well, I'm glad you suggested a ferry tour to end our day," Pleakley said. "It's breathtaking! Say, now that I think about it, shouldn't you be driving this thing?"

"This ferry is on autopilot at the moment," she said, "which makes sense. We're the only two on board, and I need to stay by your side at all times— you know, for your safety."

As she finished her sentence, Agent Weems crept up behind Pleakley and took out her vaporizing weapon.

"Right, my safety," Pleakley said with a smile. "Say, you know what would make this great moment even greater? More vanilla ice cream!"

Before Agent Weems could respond, Pleakley lunged for the ferry console. He turned off the autopilot by smashing a big red button and jumped for the control yoke, pushing forward. Immediately, the ferry went into overdrive, surging forward through the waves. Agent Weems was thrown back.

"Stop that!" Agent Weems said, trying to steady herself against the side of the ferry.

"Not until I get more ice cream!" Pleakley retorted as he banked the ferry to the right.

That threw Agent Weems off balance, and she went right over the side of the boat, dropping the vaporizer in the water.

"Sorry!" Pleakley called out as he eased up on the speed and brought the ferry around. "That was all my fault. But you know how it is when you want ice cream!"

The ferry pulled up alongside Agent Weems, and Pleakley helped her back on board.

"Well, if I didn't know before, I do now," Agent Weems said, water dripping down her nose. She nudged Pleakley away from the ferry controls and put the vehicle back on autopilot.

"You just stay away from that, before anyone gets hurt," Agent Weems said before mumbling, "like me."

"Oh, fine, no problem," Pleakley replied. "I'm an expert at staying away from things. For example— and I'll bet you didn't know this about me—I've managed to stay away from the planet Jupiter for my entire life!"

Biting her lower lip, Agent Weems said, "I'm contacting the Grand Councilwoman. I'm concerned for your safety, Pleakley. Perhaps it's time that we get you off planet, where we can keep a better eye on you."

If Pleakley was worried, he didn't show it. Instead, he looked out over the side of the ferry and said, "Look! Water!"

CHAPTER 15

As Stitch, Lilo, and Jumba emerged from the subway onto the street, they discovered they were no longer in Grand Central Terminal. Their travels must have taken them west, for they had come up right in the middle of the bustling Times Square!

It was late afternoon, the sun was going down, and the streets were full of tourists and people just getting off work. The scene was teeming with life, and in case you've never been to Times Square, it looked a little like this:

"At least we're outside," Lilo said. "Now we can—"

But before Lilo could finish, a young woman wearing a big fluffy costume that looked kind of like a blue koala bear approached.

"You can get out of my spot, that's what you can do!" the woman said.

And what's the big idea, wearin' a costume like mine? Get your own street corner!

The team walked away, and Stitch shook his head.

"Now would be good time to call GDA," Jumba said.

Stitch nodded, then reached into the gold case and produced the galactic communicator.

"Come in, GDA! Come in! Is Agent 626!" he said.

Someone on the other end replied.

"We haven't heard anything from him since he went to investigate those trash cans. I'm fearful that something might have happened. If you're telling me Toothoids are definitely involved, perhaps they've already gotten him."

"This is most awful," Jumba said. "We must do something!"

"No, you must not," Agent Peebles retorted. "The danger is too great! You are hereby ordered to stand by until I can inform the Grand Councilwoman and you receive new orders. Take no action. Do you understand?"

"Yes, but—" Stitch started.

Behind Agent Peebles, the Grand Councilwoman entered.

"Inform me of what, Agent Peebles?" she said.

"I'll update you at once," they said.

"Grand Councilwoman," Stitch started, but before he could get out another word, the transmission ended.

"That was weird," Lilo said. "It was almost like Agent Peebles didn't want us talking to the Grand Councilwoman!"

"Agent Peebles!" the small pink alien hollered. "Come on, guys, you remember me!"

"I honestly cannot," Jumba said.

"We have captured two Toothoids," Stitch said. "I will give you coordinates. Request immediate pickup!"

"Excellent work, 626," Agent Peebles said. "I'll dispatch a recovery team and notify the Grand Councilwoman. She'll want to hear your progress. And Toothoids, you say? How alarming!"

"Have you heard anything from Cobra?" Lilo asked.

"Cobra? You mean Agent Bubbles," Peebles said

"Not only that," Jumba said, "we're just supposed to stand here and do nothing? What about Pleakley?"

"Jumba's right, Stitch," Lilo said. "We can't just do nothing. Pleakley needs us!"

"Pleakley is family," Stitch said decisively. "We go get him. Now."

Without hesitation, Stitch reached into the gold case on his tool belt. He fumbled around for a moment before producing the keys to the RV. With a wide grin, Stitch pressed a red button on the key fob.

"RV will be here any minute," Stitch said. "Then we put coordinates Toothoids gave us into navigation system and save Pleakley!"

Once they boarded the RV and moved out of the way of some very annoyed New Yorkers, Stitch steered the vehicle south over the island of Manhattan while Lilo put the coordinates into the RV's navigation system.

"You're going the right way, Stitch," she affirmed as she saw a blinking dot on the screen. "At this speed, we should reach Pleakley in about two minutes!"

Stitch gave a sharp nod. "Situation will be

dangerous. Everyone, remember important detective rules. Especially this one."

Then Stitch pressed a button on the console, and the following rule popped up on the RV head-up display:

STITCH'S DETECTIVE RULE #16
stick together, work together.
A team can accomplish anything!

"Okay, the plan is we stay close and listen to each other," Lilo said.

"And each do what is necessary to remove Pleakley from danger," Jumba added.

As Stitch focused on flying the RV, Lilo turned to Jumba.

"You're really worried about Pleakley, aren't you?" she whispered.

Jumba didn't answer at first. Then he said, "Pleakley is . . . first real friend I ever had. If something happens to him, I don't know what I would do."

"Well," Lilo said, holding his hand, "then we just have to make sure that nothing *does* happen to him, right?"

Looking at Lilo, Jumba managed a slight smile. "Thank you," he said. "You . . . you are Jumba's friend, too."

Lilo looked at him, surprised. "You mean it?" she said.

Jumba nodded. "Please forgive me for things I said back in subway tunnel and thank you for not leaving me behind near small hole."

"I'm sorry about what I said, too," Lilo replied. "You really are a genius."

"And you are very kind and so, so smart," Jumba said. "I am apparently not . . . used to having friends."

"Well, you have a whole bunch now," Lilo said. "And there's one who could really use our help. So let's go get him!"

CHAPTER 16

SAVING PLEAKLEY

About two minutes later, the RV zoomed over the southern tip of Manhattan.

"There they are!" Stitch shouted, pointing ahead to a small watercraft motoring down the Hudson River. From that distance, they could see three figures standing on the ferry.

"Stay alert," Stitch said. "Remember, Toothoids can change shape. Can look like anything . . . or anyone!"

Stitch maneuvered the vehicle so it hovered directly above their target. Then he, Lilo, and Jumba slid down a ladder that extended from the RV to the deck of the ferry.

There was Pleakley! And someone they didn't recognize, dressed in the same suit as Cobra. And then there was someone else they did recognize.

"What is Grand Councilwoman doing here?" Jumba said.

"Hello friends!" Pleakley said. "I'm so glad you asked. I've been showing the Grand Councilwoman all the pictures Agent Weems and I have been taking today! Look, here's one of me on a swing!"

"Who is Agent Weems?" Lilo asked, confused.

"*I'm* Agent Weems," the woman in the dark suit with equally dark glasses said. "I work for the GDA, and Pleakley's in my protective custody. I called the Grand Councilwoman, because we got word that Toothoid imposters are running rampant."

"Yes, exactly so," the Grand Councilwoman said. "In fact, *you* might be the imposters!" She pointed at Stitch, Lilo, and Jumba.

"What?" Stitch said. "Stitch is no imposter!"

"That's what an imposter would say," Agent Weems pointed out.

"Pleakley!" Jumba shouted, reaching out for his friend. "Be careful! The Grand Councilwoman, she is fake!"

"They're both fakes, I bet!" Lilo yelled.

"Only a Toothoid would make such wild accusations as these three," interjected the Grand Councilwoman. "Those can't possibly be your friends—they're really shape-shifting aliens!"

Stitch's jaw dropped. How were they going to convince Pleakley that he, Lilo, and Jumba were the real deal, and that Agent Weems and the Grand Councilwoman were the bad guys?

"Don't listen to them, Pleakley!" Lilo yelled.

"Don't listen to them, Pleakley!" Agent Weems echoed.

"Agent Weems," the Grand Councilwoman said, "arrest those alien impersonators!"

What drama!

Indeed!

Stitch crouched low, making sure that Jumba was right behind him and that Lilo was right behind Jumba. He wasn't going down without a fight, and he would protect his friends no matter what.

He unleashed a feral growl, baring his teeth, poised for attack.

But before he could do anything . . .

"Oh, I know Agent Weems and the Grand Councilwoman are Toothoids," Pleakley said casually, as if it were entirely obvious. "I've known all along!"

"Wait, what?" Agent Weems asked.

"That's not possible!" the Grand Councilwoman interjected. "We're—we're not aliens! I mean, I am. I'm the Grand Councilwoman! But I'm not a Toothoid, and neither is Agent Weems!"

Then the Grand Councilwoman pointed at Stitch and his friends. "They're the Toothoids! Menaces, one and all!" she insisted.

"Not possible," Pleakley said.

"But how?" Agent Weems asked. "When did you figure it out?"

"Pretty much right away," Pleakley said. "Remember when we were on top of the Empire State Building and you said, 'Look, there's a giant ape'?"

Agent Weems shifted uncomfortably on her feet. "Yyyyyes," she said.

"Well, I knew then and there I was right about you. The only one smart enough to engineer something like a giant ape is Jumba! And I happened to know that Jumba hadn't done anything like that yet, because we're friends, and friends tell each other things. So if Jumba hadn't created a giant ape, then who did?"

"Nobody?" Agent Weems asked.

"That's right—nobody!" Pleakley exclaimed, practically jumping up and down. "So I realized that you had to be lying. Now, I also happen to know that GDA agents, like Cobra Bubbles, never lie. And if GDA agents don't lie, and Agent Weems told a lie, then she couldn't be a GDA agent! And therefore, Agent Weems wasn't an agent and had to be up to no good! So I decided to drag you alllllll over the city doing touristy things to keep you busy."

As Pleakley finished, he looked up to see everyone staring at him.

"Well," the fake Grand Councilwoman said, "I certainly did not predict this turn of events."

"I tried to vaporize him, multiple times," Weems complained. "But he's far too resourceful!"

In that moment, Jumba raced to Pleakley and gathered the one-eyed alien up in his burly arms. He gave Pleakley the biggest hug he could muster.

"What's this?" Pleakley said.

"I am hugging you because your deductive reasoning is most impressive!" Jumba said.

"That sounds suspiciously like a compliment," Pleakley replied with a smile.

"Of course is compliment!" Jumba said. "We give compliments to our friends."

"Is that what we are?" Pleakley asked. "Friends?"

Jumba nodded. "We are indeed. I am very, very glad that you are okay, my friend."

Now Pleakley hugged Jumba.

"Well, it doesn't matter that you figured out we are imposters," the so-called Agent Weems said. "We can't allow you to stop our plans. In mere moments, we will hypnotize all of New York City!"

"Agent Weems" pressed a button on the ferry

controls, and a crane at the back of the vehicle extended, revealing a *huge* green box.

"Behold: the much larger H.A.H.A. device!" "Agent Weems" continued. "What you saw in the subway tunnel was merely a trial run. Now that we've proved we can terraform this pitiful planet, we're moving to the next level: hypnotizing New York City! Then we'll entrance all the humans in the world! Unwittingly, they will turn Earth into a paradise for Toothoids, who will rule over all in the first phase of Project UHOP! And you will pay the price for defying us!"

Stitch and his friends let out a collective gasp. So that had been the Toothoids' plan all along!

"That was great," the "Grand Councilwoman" said as she morphed, revealing herself to be Myron, the Toothoid who had escaped from the sewers. "Good speech, Helen."

"But enough talk!" Helen sneered, changing into her Toothoid form. "We must complete our mission . . . and I'm hungry!"

It was clearly time for a . . .

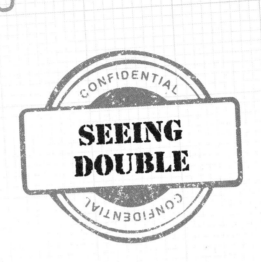

CHAPTER 17

CONFIDENTIAL

SEEING DOUBLE

CONFIDENTIAL

As Myron and Helen attacked, Stitch met them head-on. His dense body collided with the aliens, knocking them to the deck like a couple of bowling pins.

Stitch gathered himself and joined his friends as they formed a circle around the fallen Toothoids.

"Do yourself favor," Jumba said, "and don't get up."

"Oh, I'll do myself a favor, all right," Myron said. "I'm going to activate the H.A.H.A. But first I'm going to do *this!*"

Then his long, scaly tail lashed out at the ferry controls and jerked the boat hard to one side.

Unbalanced, Stitch and his companions were thrown to the deck, bumping into Myron and Helen.

Stitch quickly scrambled to his feet. But when he got back up, the Toothoids were gone.

Instead, Stitch saw something that set his mind reeling.

"Two Jumbas! Two Pleakleys!" he exclaimed. His time as a GDA agent hadn't prepared him for anything like this.

"Which ones are real?" Lilo asked.

"I'm the real Pleakley!" insisted one of the Pleakleys loudly.

But then the other Pleakley proclaimed even louder and more insistently, "No, *I'm* the real Pleakley! Obviously! Look at me: I'm a big worrywart and I think I know everything!"

"No, *I'm* a bigger worrywart and I think I know *more* everything than me! I mean, *you!*"

Meanwhile, the two Jumbas circled each other warily.

"If you are real Jumba, then tell me, what is your favorite color?" one of the Jumbas asked.

"Plaid!" the other Jumba said.

"Curses," the first Jumba muttered. "Correct!"

"This is way too confusing," Lilo said, standing next to Stitch.

But before Lilo and Stitch could try to discern the real Pleakley and Jumba for themselves, one Pleakley and one Jumba raced forward. The Pleakley tackled Stitch to the ground while the

Jumba darted to the ferry controls. The Jumba pressed a button, and the H.A.H.A. device hummed to life.

"It is done!" "Jumba" shouted. "In ten of your Earth minutes, the H.A.H.A. will be at full power. It will send out the hypnosis pulse, mesmerizing everyone in New York City!"

"Ten minutes?" Lilo asked. "Why ten minutes?"

"Look, kid, was the Most Glorious Planetary Empire of Vromblak built in a day?" "Jumba" asked. "No, no it wasn't. These things take time! You can't rush genius, and you can't make a H.A.H.A. of that size power up any faster!"

Stitch rolled to the side, escaping from underneath "Pleakley." But when he got up, he saw . . . himself!

Not only that, but there were now two Lilos!

Pleakley and Jumba stared, amazed.

"So that's what that looks like," Pleakley said.

Stitch gazed into the eyes of the Stitch imposter, then said, "That is not Stitch!"

But then the other Stitch pointed at him and said, "No, *that* is not Stitch!"

Meanwhile, the two Lilos squared off, circling each other.

"Jumba! Pleakley! It's me, Lilo! The real Lilo!" one of the Lilos said.

"No, I'm Lilo!" the other added.

Stitch realized they were in a terrible mess. The Toothoids could keep changing themselves into Stitch and his friends, confusing them, and maybe even turn them against each other.

And the team now had less than ten minutes to destroy the H.A.H.A.!

Whatever they were going to do, they were going to have to do it soon.

While he was distracted in thought, the other Stitch took a swipe at him, knocking him to the deck.

"I know you're the real you, Stitch!" Pleakley said, helping him up.

Stitch was just about to thank Pleakley when he noticed another Pleakley standing next to Jumba. The Pleakley "helping" Stitch picked up the little blue alien and threw him at the other Pleakley!

"Oof!" Stitch said as he collided with the real Pleakley.

"Ouch!" Pleakley said. "That hurts! I always forget how dense your body is!"

Then Stitch remembered one of the detective rules—the very first rule he himself had added to the list:

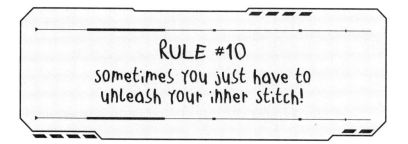

RULE #10
sometimes you just have to
unleash your inner stitch!

Stitch looked at the ferry deck and saw there were now two Jumbas and two Lilos, and a Pleakley was standing next to him. He grinned, then ran away from everyone.

"Hey, where are you going?" Pleakley called out.

Stitch didn't answer. He reached the railing on the ferry and then tumbled over the edge.

CHAPTER 18

CONFIDENTIAL

'OHANA

CONFIDENTIAL

You're probably still reeling from all the drama of
the last chapter, especially that ending. Well, then
you won't mind if we pile on even more drama! *Say
it with us . . .*

"Stitch, no!" one of the Lilos cried.

"His body is far too dense!" a Jumba said. "If 626 hits water, he will sink like . . . like . . . very heavy thing that sinks!"

As fast as they could, one of the Lilos and one of the Jumbas joined the real Pleakley in practically diving over the side of the ferry to try to grab Stitch before he could land in the water below.

But when they reached the side of the ferry and looked over, here's what they saw:

Hello, real friends!

Then, using the great strength contained in his tiny limbs, Stitch flipped himself up from the hull of the ferry and back onto the deck. He now stood with Pleakley, and the *real* Lilo and Jumba were behind him. For a moment, they huddled together, whispering. Then they turned, as a team, to face the Toothoids.

"These are my friends," Stitch said as he stared at the other Lilo and Jumba, who were advancing on him. "You are fakes. Toothoids. And you have lost."

"*We* haven't lost anything," the fake Lilo said. She morphed back into Myron. "We have you right where we want you!"

And then a computerlike voice came from the device at the back of the ferry.

"Five minutes until H.A.H.A.," the voice said.

"Five minutes!" Myron exclaimed. "Five minutes until your doom!"

Behind Stitch, the real Lilo let out a chuckle. "I think it might be the other way around," she said as she gave Stitch a knowing look.

Stitch smiled and dove into Myron. As the two fought, tumbling end over end, the real Stitch remained himself. But Myron? Myron kept on changing form, trying to disorient Agent 626.

Did it work? Not even close. There was no way Stitch was going to allow himself to be distracted. Not now. He held tight to Myron. And regardless of what the Toothoid turned himself into, Agent 626 kept holding on.

"Why . . . won't . . . you . . . let . . . go?" Myron said, struggling to free himself from Stitch's iron grip.

"Because you threatened my friends," Stitch said. "My 'ohana. And no one messes with Stitch's family."

They rolled all around the ferry deck until, at last, Myron fell down, exhausted.

"You may have beaten me," Myron said, "but you can't stop the H.A.H.A.!"

Stitch sprang up onto his feet and turned to see Lilo, Jumba, and Pleakley cornering "Agent Weems."

"Great job, Stitch!" Lilo said. "You took down Myron, and we got Agent Weems!"

"Agent Weems" morphed back into her Toothoid form.

"It's Helen, please," she said. "All right, you've got

me. You know, I never really liked our whole plan to begin with."

Stitch was digging around in his case and pulled out what looked like a length of red rope.

"Here," Stitch said, handing it to Jumba. "Tie them up!"

Jumba did so without hesitation.

The alien scientist was about to say something when the computer voice cut through the air. "Two minutes to H.A.H.A," it announced.

At once, Stitch ran back to the device, and Lilo followed, while Jumba and Pleakley kept watch over the defeated Toothoids. Stitch pressed the button, but nothing happened.

"How can we stop it, Stitch?" Lilo asked. Stitch tried pressing the button again.

"H.A.H.A. imminent," the computer voice said. "Enjoy your hypnosis."

The button wasn't working! A few seconds passed, and then Stitch said, "Stitch has an idea. But we must work together."

"Working together is what we do," Lilo said. "We're a team, right?"

"Right!" Stitch replied. "Everyone, get to RV!"

Without a word, Jumba and Pleakley gathered the Toothoids and took them up the ladder to the RV.

"You too, Lilo," Stitch said, pushing her to the ladder as he whispered something in her ear.

"Are you sure?" Lilo said in disbelief.

"Stitch is sure," 626 replied. "Now go!"

"Ten . . ." came the voice from the H.A.H.A. "Nine . . . eight . . ."

"Climb, Lilo, climb!" Stitch shouted as he turned to face the H.A.H.A.

". . . seven . . . six . . ."

Once he saw Lilo and the others safely aboard the RV, Stitch jumped straight up in the air as high as he could. And then . . .

Stitch had done it! The H.A.HA. had crashed into the ship. It was now useless.

The boat sank almost immediately . . . and Stitch along with it.

CHAPTER 19

Fortunately, however, Stitch and Lilo already had a plan!

The moment Stitch hit the water, the RV zoomed down, and the door opened. Jumba held on to Lilo, who grabbed on to Stitch. Then Jumba and Lilo yanked as hard as they could, bringing Stitch aboard the RV.

"Thanks, Lilo!" Stitch said, shaking the water off his fur.

"Good teamwork, group!" Lilo said, giving everyone a thumbs-up.

Helen gave the thumbs-up back.

Myron shoved Helen's arm. "Why are you giving them the thumbs-up?" he asked, annoyed.

"I thought they wanted me to," Helen said.

"No, they don't want you to," Myron grumbled. "Well, forget the Toothoid invasion now. Ugh, I hate it when my plans fail. My bad."

Then Pleakley approached Helen.

"I believe you know what I want," Pleakley said.

With a heavy sigh, Helen handed over Pleakley's guidebook.

"Welcome back!" Pleakley said, and he kissed the book. "I never thought I'd see you again!"

With the Toothoids defeated, Stitch was at last able to cross the third item off on his checklist:

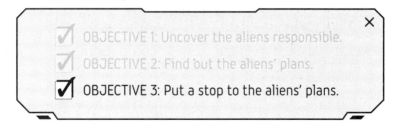

×

OBJECTIVE 1: Uncover the aliens responsible.

OBJECTIVE 2: Find out the aliens' plans.

OBJECTIVE 3: Put a stop to the aliens' plans.

Stitch looked at the fallen Toothoids and then at his friends. "Case solved," he said.

"What do we do now?" Lilo asked.

"I think we have our answer," Jumba said as he pointed out the windshield to the sky, "up there."

Yay!

Case solved!

In the distance, and rapidly approaching, was a small red spacecraft. Something about it seemed familiar to Stitch. It looked like the same spacecraft in which he had escaped from the Galactic Federation, before crash-landing on Earth!

The RV landed in a park on the shore, and soon the red craft followed. The hatch opened, and out walked Cobra Bubbles.

"Welcome back, Agent Bubbles!" Lilo said as she showed off the captured Toothoids.

"I see you've been busy," Cobra said. "Meanwhile, I was on a wild-goose chase."

"Wild-goose chase?" Jumba said. "Why would anyone want to chase wild geese?"

"I chased a wild goose once," Pleakley said. "Well, it was kind of the other way around."

"Anyway," Cobra said, "I went downtown, and there was nothing out of the ordinary there. Either I missed whatever happened, or it was just a Toothoid ruse designed to separate me from you."

"Yes, yes! It was that last one! And it worked, too!" Myron sneered. But then his face fell. "Not that it did us any good."

"No, you messed with the wrong agent. Fortunately, I was able to request this old ship to come find you all," Cobra said, looking at Stitch. "Nice work, 626."

Myron stared right at Stitch's eyes. "I need to know," he said. "Back on the ferry, how did you figure out who was who?"

Stitch walked over to Myron. "It was simple," Agent 626 said. "Stitch put himself in danger. Only friends would try to save him."

Myron smiled. "Elegant," the Toothoid said. "The one thing we hadn't counted on was . . . friendship."

"The one thing you hadn't counted on was Agent 626," Lilo said, correcting him.

"Yes, that, too," Myron replied. "So two things, I guess. I never was very good at counting."

Then Stitch turned to face Cobra, agent to agent.

"Let's contact the Grand Councilwoman," Cobra said, "let her know our job here is done."

"Sounds good," Stitch said.

Cobra turned the dial on his watch, and the hologram of the Grand Councilwoman appeared, with Agent Peebles standing next to her.

"Greetings, Agent Bubbles, Agent 626," the Grand Councilwoman said. "What news do you have?"

"Agent 626, will you deliver the report?" Cobra said, deferring to Stitch.

Stitch gave a nod. "Grand Councilwoman," he began, "we have foiled the plans of the Toothoids. Have captured them all."

"Well done, agents!" the Grand Councilwoman exclaimed. It was rare for her to show any emotion. "Yes, Cobra had informed us about the Toothoids! We're lucky that you were able to stop them. With their shape-shifting abilities, they can be exceptionally difficult to locate, let alone apprehend."

Then the Grand Councilwoman looked at Agent Peebles.

"Dispatch a prison ship to Earth to pick up the

Toothoid prisoners," the Grand Councilwoman said. "See to it personally, Agent Peebles. We cannot allow them to escape. We must learn more about their plans."

"Yes, Grand Councilwoman!" Agent Peebles said as they raced out of sight to carry out the orders.

"I will interrogate those Toothoids personally," the Grand Councilwoman said.

"They were trying to terraform Earth," Lilo explained. "Something about changing the environment of this planet to one that could support Toothoid life."

"Curious," the Grand Councilwoman replied. "I wonder why."

"When I spoke with the Toothoids, they mentioned a leader . . . an Exalted One," Stitch said. "And something about UHOP."

The Grand Councilwoman thought for a moment. "We have heard mentions of these both before but have little information."

"UHOP? We thought UHOP was a pancake place," Lilo said. "But maybe . . . maybe it's something else?"

"Do you think . . . it is connected to the Snailiens?" Stitch asked.

"Snailiens . . . and Toothoids . . . working together?" Cobra said.

"The thought is too horrible," the Grand Councilwoman said. "And yet we must consider it. Two major attacks on Earth, within days of each other, carried out by hostile alien forces? Both preparing the way for an invasion? Agents, I fear the worst may be yet to come."

"Then Agent 626 will be ready," Stitch said as he saluted the Grand Councilwoman before turning to his friends. "*We* will be ready."

"I know you will," the Grand Councilwoman replied. "Thank you, everyone. Your service continues to make the galaxy a safer place. I will be in touch soon with your next assignment."

Then the hologram faded from view.

The Galactic Federation prison ship appeared about an hour later to pick up Myron and Helen from the ferry. Thanks to the coordinates Stitch had provided earlier, they had already collected the two Toothoids in the subway tunnel.

Meanwhile, Cobra climbed back aboard the red spacecraft.

"You'd better get back to the RV," he said to the others. "I'm gonna activate a tractor beam and see if I can fish that ferry out of the water."

"Yes, this 'ferry' looked to be of Toothoid design," Jumba said. "It might be interesting to take apart, see what makes their technology tick."

Cobra nodded. "When the time comes, I'll make sure you're there to lend a hand, Jumba."

Jumba smiled. "Would be nice to work in a lab

again. You know, not making incredibly destructive creatures capable of leveling entire cities."

"Uh, yeah," Cobra said. "Anyway, it's about time I—"

"Oh, no!"

Everyone turned to look at Lilo. She seemed to be in a panic.

"Lilo, what is it?" Cobra asked, concerned.

"I just realized," Lilo said as she looked at Cobra and Stitch, "I haven't spoken with Nani in forever!"

"Hasn't technically been 'forever,'" Jumba said. "It has only been day."

"True," Pleakley said. "'Forever' would be . . . well, forever!"

Well said.

"No need to worry," Cobra said. "Before I met up with you, I called Nani. Updated her on everything."

"You mean . . . everything?" Lilo said with a loud gulp. "Like . . . *everything* everything?"

All Lilo could think about now was how much trouble she was going to be in. Nani would be absolutely furious with her if she knew that Lilo had been running all over New York City fighting Toothoids!

"Lilo, I'm kidding," Cobra said, and he smiled at the girl. "I told Nani that you were fine, and that you're staying with me for a few days. That is technically true, because I'm gonna be keeping tabs on you and your crew until our next assignment."

Lilo let out the biggest sigh of relief in the history of sighs of relief. "Thanks, Cobra," she said.

"Anytime," Cobra replied. "See you soon."

Cobra closed the cockpit on the red spaceship as Lilo, Stitch, Jumba, and Pleakley climbed back aboard the RV.

"You wanna keep following them?"

"I rather think I've had enough. Back to the subway, darling?"

Inside the RV, Stitch watched as Cobra activated the tractor beam. The ship hovered over the water for a moment before it seemed to lock on to something. A second later, Cobra flew off, with the waterlogged Toothoid ferry in tow.

"Stitch wants to say thank you," he said, turning to his friends. "I behaved . . . badly before. I should have trusted you more. You are my team, now and always. Even more, you are my family."

"We're sorry you didn't think we trusted you, Stitch," Lilo said. "You're amazing."

"So are you," Jumba said, pointing at Pleakley.

"Right back at you!" Pleakley replied with a smile.

"Well, we have a little downtime before next assignment," Jumba said. "Where to?"

"I'd like to see a Broadway show!" Lilo said. "Something with a lot of singing and dancing!"

"Me too!" Pleakley exclaimed. "Let's get dressed up! I've got just the wig!"

"Broadway it is," Stitch said as he flew the RV uptown for an evening of well-earned fun.

The End ...?

Okay, so apparently that wasn't the end. Well, it was the end, but not *the* end. That's because there's more book left.

Back aboard the Grand Councilwoman's ship, there was much concern.

"This is most troubling," said the Grand Councilwoman.

She couldn't stop thinking about the possibility of the Toothoids working with the Snailiens. An alliance such as that could well spell disaster for the Galactic Federation. And it could mean certain doom for Earth.

And then the mention of an "Exalted One" and "UHOP"?

There were many pieces to the mystery, and nothing yet seemed to fit together.

"I will be in my chambers, consulting with the council," she said. "Agent Peebles, please notify me as soon as the Toothoid prisoners arrive. I will deal with them directly."

"Yes, Grand Councilwoman," Agent Peebles replied.

The Grand Councilwoman left the control room as Agent Peebles leaned back in their chair. A moment later, they saw an incoming transmission from the prison ship on their view screen. The Toothoid prisoners had been collected, and the prison ship would be returning shortly.

Agent Peebles looked over their shoulder, watching as the Grand Councilwoman walked down the hallway to her chambers.

Then Agent Peebles switched off their view screen. They then took out a small egg-shaped device and twisted the top from the bottom. The device opened, revealing a small screen. Agent Peebles could see a shadowy figure on the screen.

"Greetings, Exalted One," Agent Peebles said. "It is my unfortunate duty to inform you that both the Snailiens and the Toothoids have failed to pave the way for Operation: UHOP. Despite my attempts to interfere in their investigation, Agent 626 and his team have thwarted all efforts so far."

"I see," said the shadowy figure. "We are . . . displeased."

"But there is still hope," Agent Peebles replied. "We have made contact with another group of aliens. Already they make their preparations in a place called South Korea."

"This is good news," the Exalted One said. "It means you may live another day. And Operation: UHOP shall yet succeed."

"Success," the traitorous Agent Peebles said.

"Success," the Exalted One replied before the screen went dark.

ACKNOWLEDGMENTS

Simply put, writing this book has been a dream.
I love *Lilo & Stitch*—it's one of my all-time favorite
films. I love the characters (wish I was Stitch, but
I'm definitely Pleakley). So I can't thank my editor,
Holly P. Rice, enough. Without Holly's creativity and
enthusiastic editorial vision, this book wouldn't
exist. I'd also like to thank Elana Cohen, who
suggested me for this project in the first place.
Last, an enormous thank you to my wife, Nina, who
might just love *Lilo & Stitch* more than I do. Now
if you'll excuse me, I'm off to deliver this peanut-
butter sandwich to Pudge.

ABOUT THE AUTHOR

Steve Behling would take the red ship, likes Elvis, and sinks in water but swears he is not an alien. Regardless, he's written the completely bonkers junior novel adaptation of *Dora and the Lost City of Gold* and the original middle-grade novels *Avengers Endgame: The Pirate Angel, the Talking Tree, and Captain Rabbit* and *Onward: The Search for the Phoenix Gem*, to name a few. Steve lives in a top-secret subterranean lair with his wife, two human children, and three-legged wonder beagle, Loomis.

ABOUT THE ILLUSTRATOR

Arianna Rea slipped into Disney movies as a child. With the help of her magical friends, she managed to find the keys to Wonderland and get back to her drawing desk in Rome, Italy, where she lives, to illustrate her heroes' adventures in the Disney book series Princess Beginnings and Before the Story. She will draw anything: from restaurant placemats and menus to illustrated books, comic books like *Inside Out,* and cartoon characters like Disney's Star Darlings. However, she doesn't just draw cute characters: lately, she's been having this weird passion for aliens . . . perhaps due to Stitch's irresistible charm.